The Magic Cake Shop

by Meika Hashimoto

illustrations by Josée Masse

RANDOM HOUSE 🏠 NEW YORK

Text copyright © 2011 by Meika Hashimoto
Jacket art and interior illustrations copyright © 2011 by Josée Masse

Visit us on the Web! www.randomhouse.com/teens

Educators and librarians, for a variety of teaching tools, visit us at www.randomhouse.com/teachers

Library of Congress Cataloging-in-Publication Data
Hashimoto, Meika.
The magic cake shop / by Meika Hashimoto ; illustrations by Josée Masse. — 1st ed.
p. cm.
Summary: When ten-year-old Emma Burblee's beautiful but snobbish parents banish her to Nummington for the summer with her loathsome Uncle Simon, she is befriended by the seemingly magical town baker, Mr. Crackle, who soon becomes a target of Simon and his cohort.
ISBN 978-0-375-86822-1 (trade) — ISBN 978-0-375-96822-8 (lib. bdg.) — ISBN 978-0-375-89874-7 (ebook)
[1. Bakers and bakeries—Fiction. 2. Magic—Fiction. 3. Conduct of life—Fiction. 4. Uncles—Fiction.] I. Masse, Josée, ill. II. Title.
PZ7.H27Mag 2011 [Fic]—dc22 2010041098

Printed in the United States of America

10 9 8 7 6 5 4 3 2

First Edition

For
Nori Hashimoto,
who loves dessert even more
than his bigger sister

Contents

✴ 1 ✴

Meet the Burblees

Mr. and Mrs. Burblee were very beautiful. Mrs. Burblee had a delicate chin, dainty earlobes, and a charming smile. Mr. Burblee had a rugged chin, manly earlobes, and a winning smile.

When Mrs. Burblee went for a walk, many a man tripped over his feet in a rush to say hello. If Mrs. Burblee said hello back, the goggle-eyed man usually fell off the sidewalk, sometimes into oncoming traffic.

Mrs. Burblee took this as a compliment.

When Mr. Burblee took a ride on his motorcycle, he liked to grin at the lady drivers at stoplights. They usually fainted. In the past year, Mr. Burblee had been responsible for eighty-two traffic jams.

He liked to keep count.

From the moment they opened their dazzling eyes in the morning to their eighty-step face-washing ritual before bed, the Burblees busied themselves with powdering, perfuming, and polishing. When they weren't applying lotion or slicking hair or beautifying themselves in hundreds of ways, they bickered over who got to be admired.

"What shall we talk about today?" Mr. Burblee asked Mrs. Burblee one morning over a breakfast of carrots and celery. "Shall it be the noble shape of my nose or my fabulously silky locks of hair?"

Mrs. Burblee pouted her rosy lips and frowned. "We talked about your hair yesterday. It's my turn. I want to compose poems about the graceful curves of my feet."

"As long as it's my nose tomorrow," Mr. Burblee huffed, sinking his pearly teeth into a celery stick.

For the rest of the day, they wrote odes to Mrs. Burblee's feet.

The Burblees lived in a fancy apartment building named Stoney Henge in a wildly expensive part of the city. Stoney Henge was built of solid steel and granite. High-heeled women clacked their way through the lobby night and day, while loud-talking men in suits bragged about their latest business deal. The elevator buttons were lined with diamonds that had a nasty habit of nicking fingers.

Inside the Burblees' apartment, expensive furniture was perfectly arranged throughout each room. In the dining room, gold-encrusted stone-hard chairs made for stylish but uncomfortable mealtimes. Snarling gargoyles in the bathroom stared at anyone who entered and made it difficult to do one's business.

In the Burblees' bedroom, gigantic dressers stuffed

with Mr. Burblee's designer socks stood next to shelves full of Mrs. Burblee's nail products. Deep closets opened up to a carefully arranged onslaught of accessories, including Mr. Burblee's prize collection of polka-dot ties and Mrs. Burblee's three hundred pairs of earmuffs.

The spare room next door held nothing but clothes.

The Burblees had lived in Stoney Henge ever since Mr. Burblee made millions off a fancy hat boutique called Chic-Chic. The boutique was the sort that had tall, thin-lipped clerks with pointy noses that they would stick up if you didn't enter the shop with the latest style of purse or sunglasses. Chic-Chic decorated hats with things like hummingbirds and mousetraps and insisted the models be photographed in places like Mozambique and Antarctica. This was supposed to make the hats seem more fashionable.

Mr. Burblee was very good at bringing customers to Chic-Chic. "The trick," he boasted to Mrs. Burblee one night at dinner, "is to make women feel rotten about themselves. Once you make them feel ugly, they'll be desperate to buy anything that seems to make them instantly beautiful."

"Is that so?" murmured Mrs. Burblee, picking daintily at her lettuce.

"Remember that commercial I ran on television last year? The one where I painted zits on your nose and warts on your cheeks and had you wear that hideous wig with gray streaks?"

"And then you had me wander into Chic-Chic, put on a hat, and transform into my usual ravishing self? Yes, I remember—I was there," said Mrs. Burblee with a touch of irritation. "You never stop talking about that commercial. I know it was a success and we made a fortune, but you really had nothing to do with it."

"Of course I did! I came up with the idea!" sputtered Mr. Burblee.

"But I was the model. Without me, no one would have remembered your idea. My irresistible beauty is the reason why Chic-Chic is so popular." Mrs. Burblee smiled and primped her hair.

Mr. Burblee scowled.

"Don't scowl—you'll get wrinkles," said Mrs. Burblee.

They finished the rest of their dinner in silence.

In addition to being a model for Chic-Chic, once a week Mrs. Burblee pumped up sales by working behind the counter at the boutique. She was very good at charming hordes of men into buying pricey eggbeater or porcelain hats. "Trust me," Mrs. Burblee would coo to a male customer, "your wife will love it." She would give him a smoldering look, and before he knew it, the befuddled man would have his credit card swiped and his hands full of a hatbox.

Chic-Chic had a no-return, no-refund policy.

Working together, the Burblees did ripping good business. Mrs. Burblee bamboozled men into handing over their wallets, and Mr. Burblee's commercials brought in women desperate to seem fashionable at any cost.

Chic-Chic allowed the Burblees to live a life of complete luxury. They drank fancy champagne and ate rare caviar by the gallon. Mrs. Burblee had a jewelry box stuffed with emeralds and pearls. Mr. Burblee kept his seventeen yachts in the most expensive boathouse in the city. Together they owned a small island in a fashionable part of the Pacific Ocean.

But despite their wildly good looks and fortune, the Burblees had one great, terrible blot on their dipped-in-gold world.

✦ 2 ✦

Emma

In their opinions, Mr. and Mrs. Burblee had the perfect, most beautiful life—except for one annoying detail.

That detail was a little girl called Emma.

Emma was Mr. and Mrs. Burblee's daughter. When Mrs. Burblee saw her baby for the first time, she shuddered. "Gracious, I do hope she grows into something more becoming."

Mr. Burblee glanced at Emma's straight brown hair, smatter of freckles, and steady brown eyes. He patted his wife's hand. "Don't worry, darling. She's sure to become a stunner." He poked at a freckle on Emma's face. "And if she doesn't turn into a first-rate beauty, there's sure to be surgery and operations to fix her."

But Emma did not turn into an angelic vision of loveliness. Her teeth grew in slightly crooked. Her freckles increased year by year. Her hair stayed straight. Her eyes remained brown and steady—though as she grew older, they developed a glint of fire.

Emma gave her parents more headaches than they could count. Every time Mr. and Mrs. Burblee tried a beauty treatment on her, she found a way to undo their efforts. She refused to have her teeth straightened or her ears pierced or her eyebrows plucked. When Mrs. Burblee dragged her to a salon to curl her hair, Emma kicked the stylist and got banned from the salon. When Mr. Burblee bought her an uncomfortably stylish dress for her sixth birthday, it was found three days later in the local pet shop. Someone had neatly shredded the dress into bedding for the display puppies to nap in.

Emma never kept her dresses clean and wore pants when Mrs. Burblee wasn't looking. She avoided baths and toothpaste like the plague. Much to her parents' horror, she did not dive into a world of nail polish and lipstick and glamour products. Instead, she spent most of her time digging for buried treasure in the park with Charles, the Burblees' chauffeur.

Not only did Emma drive her parents nuts by not caring about her looks, but she also bothered them with the Troubles of the World. One day she came home from school, her face flushed with anger. Mrs. Burblee took one look at her daughter and said, "Emma, you look horrible! Your face is all splotchy."

"Mom, guess what I learned today!" Emma threw down her book bag and stood shaking with fury.

"Well, for heaven's sake, be less loud when you're mad— it'll ruin your vocal cords. And you have *got* to learn how to look angry without your face turning into a pepperoni pie—it's unladylike."

"Did you know that every five seconds a child dies of hunger?"

Mrs. Burblee paused. "Who told you that?"

"Ms. Bailey, my social studies teacher."

Mrs. Burblee sighed. "First of all, you should not be upset over something so silly. Why, some mothers I know would just *die* to be as thin as starving children. And second of all, I *refuse* to have a teacher make my daughter look like a blotchy, splotchy mess. I'm calling your principal right away and having that awful woman fired." Mrs. Burblee took out her phone, hunted for a number, then pressed a button.

"That is not the point!" Emma said.

Mrs. Burblee frowned. "Hello, Principal Jenkins? Yes, this is Emma Burblee's mother. I need to have a word with you about Ms. Bailey."

Emma went silently to her room. That night, she logged on to her computer and did some research. The next morning, she emptied the lipstick-shaped bank that her parents had stuffed with money and given to her on her last birthday ("for plastic surgery when you turn eleven," they had said) and mailed every crisp bill to End World Hunger, a group that gave food to thousands of people around the globe.

The next day at school, Emma found Principal Jenkins and got her to promise not to fire Ms. Bailey in exchange for an extra-fancy Chic-Chic hat.

✳ 3 ✳

Chocolate Lover's Delight

When Emma displayed no interest in fashion, Mr. and Mrs. Burblee were terribly displeased. When she gave her allowance to street musicians instead of spending gobs of money on makeup and perfume, they fretted and frumped.

But what drove Mr. and Mrs. Burblee absolutely, maddeningly batty was Emma's endless curiosity about food.

Mr. and Mrs. Burblee regarded most food with horror and revulsion. Mr. Burblee liked nothing better than a tiny meal of carrots and water. Mrs. Burblee carried around a little vial of vinegar that she sniffed from if she had to pass a bakery or sweet shop. "Vulgar, nasty places," she would mutter. If Emma was with her, Mrs. Burblee would force her to sniff from the vial as well.

When Emma was four, the Burblees hired a fashionable cook named Mrs. Piffle to prepare their daily meals. Mrs. Piffle was a slim woman with sharp eyes and clawlike hands who ruthlessly banned anything that smacked of sugar or butter. She kept the Burblees on a strict low-calorie diet and forbade Emma from eating outside the home.

Every time Emma came back from an outing, she was forced to stand in front of Mrs. Piffle with her mouth wide open. Mrs. Piffle would take a deep sniff, and if she detected even a whiff of candy or sweets, she sent Emma to her room without supper.

On Emma's first day of kindergarten, Mrs. Piffle handed her a small bag. "This is your lunch. You are forbidden to eat anything else," she warned.

Emma gave the bag a shake. It was featherlight. "What if my teacher gives me cookies for snack time? Can I eat them?" she asked.

"Absolutely not!" Mrs. Piffle shrieked. "Cookies are for children with no willpower who grow up to be hideous blimps." In a high-pitched voice, she crowed, "Remember, you'll only win if you're model-thin!"

"Quite right," Mrs. Burblee agreed, patting Emma's cheek. "Have a lovely day at kindergarten, dear!" she called before flouncing out to go to Chic-Chic.

When Emma opened the bag in the school cafeteria, she found a Tupperware full of bits of kale and cauliflower, cobbled together with a nub of cheese.

"Eeew, what's that?" asked a girl sitting next to her.

Emma nudged a cauliflower bit. "I'm not sure." She hungrily glanced at the girl's peanut butter and jelly sandwich. "Want to trade?"

The girl wrinkled her nose. "No! Gross! Your lunch

smells funny. Hey, everyone," she bellowed. "Come look at Emma's stinky lunch!"

"Oh, grooosss!"

"Hey, aren't you the kid who won't eat cookies at snack time? You're weeeeird!"

"Is that alien food? Are you an alien?"

As her classmates crowded around, Emma felt herself shrink lower and lower into her seat. Kindergarten was going to be a long year with Mrs. Piffle's Tupperware lunches.

One wintry day, Mrs. Burblee arrived home and tossed a wrinkled paper bag on the living room table. Emma, who was quietly gluing together a paper model airplane, looked up. Her mother was eyeing the bag the way a gardener eyeballs a slug chewing on his best head of lettuce.

"Of all the most insulting things!" Mrs. Burblee cried.

Mr. Burblee came out of the bedroom, adjusting his newest tie. "What's wrong, dear?" he asked.

Mrs. Burblee pointed a trembling finger at the rumpled bag. "What's wrong is this unsightly Christmas gift Mrs. Finklepop just gave me!"

"Who's Mrs. Finklepop?" Emma asked.

Mr. Burblee frowned down at his tie. "Isn't she that woman who buys a Chic-Chic hat each week?"

"That *pudgy* woman who buys a Chic-Chic hat each week." Mrs. Burblee shuddered. "I try to be extra-nice to her since she is a regular customer, but just *look* at the disgusting thing she gave me this afternoon!"

Emma put down the glue and airplane and scooted over to the table. She opened the paper bag and pulled out a book. *The Chocolate Lover's Delight* was written in gold cursive on the front.

"A DESSERT COOKBOOK! THAT AWFUL WOMAN GAVE ME A *DESSERT* COOKBOOK!" Mrs. Burblee bawled. "She thinks I like to eat fat-stuffed, sugar-jacked, high-calorie filth!"

"What a wretched woman," Mr. Burblee said, fiddling with his tie.

"Disgusting," Mrs. Burblee agreed. She flounced over to Emma. With her index finger and thumb, she plucked the book from Emma's hands. Holding the book as if it were a moldy grape, she carried it to the trash and dropped it in. "Emma, be a dear and take out the garbage. I can't stand the thought of that book in my home for one more instant."

As Emma wiped her hands and got up, Mrs. Burblee marched to the bathroom. "I need a shower to rid myself of the vileness of touching that thing," she announced, then disappeared.

Mr. Burblee lifted his eyebrows, then went into the bedroom to work on his tie knot.

Emma went to the trash bin and hefted up the plastic bag with the book. She carried it out of the apartment and into the hallway to the trash chute. She was just about to drop the bag into the chute when a nudge of curiosity got the better of her.

She looked left and right.

No one was there.

The hallway was cool and silent.

Emma sat down and reached into the trash bag. Her hand closed on the dessert book. With a quick tug, she removed it from the plastic bag.

Nervously, she ran her fingers over the embossed gold letters on the cover. She opened the book to the first recipe. Her heart gave a tiny jump.

She was staring at a photograph of a five-layered slice of chocolate cake, drizzled in icing and topped with a ripe red strawberry.

Emma turned the page. It held a recipe for chocolate cream pie. Tiny sprinkles of grated dark chocolate floated on clouds of whipped cream that rested on a light brown bed of chocolate custard.

Emma felt her head spin as she looked at the picture. As she turned each glossy, chocolate-filled page, she felt like she had discovered a magic spell book. Words like "mix" and "fold" and "melt" leaped out like secret words of power. She spent the evening in her room, tracing the recipe directions with her finger, trying to make sense of the words and how they could create each breathtaking dessert pictured on the opposite page. For the next two months she read and reread the cookbook, waiting for her chance to dodge Mrs. Piffle and try out her first dessert recipe.

One Saturday morning, Mrs. Piffle fell ill with the flu,

leaving the Burblees to cook for themselves. Mr. and Mrs. Burblee harrumphed and comforted themselves with a bag of baby carrots from the refrigerator before heading to Chic-Chic.

Emma, however, had other plans. Trembling with anticipation, she dug out *The Chocolate Lover's Delight* from underneath her bed. With a fistful of her allowance clutched tightly in her pocket, she made a trip to the grocery store and came back with ingredients for chocolate cream pie. She spent the afternoon stirring and mixing and sifting, feverishly baking her first homemade dessert. Mindful of Mrs. Piffle's wrath, she cleaned up her dishes and put them back exactly as she had found them while the pie baked in the oven.

When the Burblees arrived back at the apartment, Mrs. Burblee let out an ear-piercing shriek. "It smells like fat and sugar in here!" she cried.

Emma emerged from the kitchen, proudly holding a wobbly brown chocolate cream pie. "Mom! Dad! I just made my first dessert!"

Mr. Burblee looked horrified. He stared at his young daughter as though she had grown an extra nose. "Emma Burblee, do you *know* how many calories are in dessert? Do you *know* how long you would have to starve yourself to lose all the weight you would gain if you *ate* that abomination?"

"Quite right," Mrs. Burblee chimed. "Now give me that hideous thing so I can throw it away immediately!"

Emma's smile faded. She looked at her stylish, thin parents. Her heart fell.

Mrs. Burblee advanced on her daughter, her arms outstretched to grab the pie.

In one swift motion, Emma dipped her hand into the cream and stuffed it into her mouth.

Mr. Burblee yelped. He darted over and yanked the pie out of Emma's hands. Mrs. Burblee began to sob hysterically. She pulled out her cell phone and punched buttons. "I'm calling Mrs. Piffle right now! She is never allowed to get sick again. From now on, if she's not around, you, Emma Burblee, will eat nothing but radishes!"

Emma watched as Mr. Burblee dumped her first dessert into the trash. "Now go to your room and think about what you have done!" her father roared.

Emma went to her room and sat very, very still for a long, long time.

The next day she went to the library and staggered home with seventeen cookbooks, sneaking them into her room while her parents were at work. Though Mr. and Mrs. Burblee forbade her to use the kitchen ever again (and Mrs. Piffle grimly enforced their rule), they could not prevent Emma from secretly poring over recipes for hours on end. She memorized cooking conversions and the best cookie-baking temperatures. She decorated her room with teaspoons and spatulas and cookie cutters.

When Charles heard of Emma's newest obsession, he

started picking up dessert magazines for her. Emma took the limo home from school every afternoon, and it was always a happy surprise when Charles pulled up to the school parking lot with a big grin and the latest edition of *Sweet Tooth* in his hand.

After three months of haggling, Emma convinced her parents to let her take cooking classes. They agreed only after the instructor promised to teach strictly low-fat recipes, and Emma promised to take modeling classes as well.

"But," Mr. Burblee warned, "you are not allowed to taste or eat anything you make."

Mrs. Burblee added, "And if you *ever* make another cream pie or dessert"—here she daintily swooned but recovered herself—"you will spend each evening for the next month counting your calorie intake with Mrs. Piffle."

Though she was never allowed into the kitchen at home again, Emma dreamed and planned and hoped for the day when she could move far, far away from her parents and learn to bake every kind of dessert.

⋆ 4 ⋆

Mrs. Burblee's Plan

One rainy afternoon shortly before school ended, Emma came home with her finger smarting. It was the third time that week she had accidentally scraped herself on the elevator button. When she opened the front door, she saw her mother standing there with a lovely smile on her face.

Emma sensed trouble.

"Mom, do we have Band-Aids? I cut myself." Emma held out her finger.

"Darling, do you know what next Saturday is?" Mrs. Burblee's smile widened. Her polished teeth gleamed.

"Yup. It's my birthday. I need to clean this cut," said Emma, and headed toward the bathroom.

Her mother followed. "It *is* your birthday!" Mrs. Burblee's voice sang with excitement. "And it's your *tenth* birthday, Emma. Do you know what that means?"

"A birthday party?" Emma stood over the sink and twisted the handle. A hiss of cold water ran over her finger.

"It means a *dinner party,* darling! With all of our friends here to see just how much you've grown!"

Emma dried her finger and hunted through the medicine cabinet for the Band-Aids. "Couldn't I just have a party in the park with my friends and no grown-ups?" There were no Band-Aids in sight.

Mrs. Burblee's lightbulb smile lost a few watts. "Of course not! How are your father and I supposed to show you off if we don't invite our own friends?"

"Mom, you said I look plain and ordinary. Why would you want your friends to see me? And have you seen any Band-Aids?" Emma closed the cabinet doors.

Mrs. Burblee sighed. "We do not have Band-Aids. Graceful people like your father and myself are never clumsy enough to hurt ourselves."

Emma gritted her teeth and went to the kitchen, where she found a roll of paper towels. She tore off a piece and pressed it against her finger. She found a rubber band and wrapped it around the towel to hold it in place.

Mrs. Burblee watched her worriedly. "I do hope that finger of yours heals by Saturday. You need to look perfect for our guests."

Emma exploded. "Mom! I am not perfect and I do not look perfect. And I don't care!"

Mrs. Burblee's voice suddenly became low and hard and very, very cold. "Emma, this party means a lot to your father and me. You *will* look stunning for this party. I have already ordered your dress. Saturday morning we will go shoe shopping and find you some proper heels. You have a hair appointment at ten. You are forbidden to kick the stylist. At noon you will have your nails manicured and your feet pedicured. At three my makeup artist will do your face. Afterward, we will go home. You will not rip your dress. You will not muss your makeup. You will do nothing to look less than perfect. The party is at six."

Emma cringed. "I have to stay in my dress with makeup on all afternoon?"

"Yes. And"—Mrs. Burblee's voice became even frostier—"if you complain or do anything to embarrass your father and me, you will spend your summer vacation at your uncle's instead of going horseback riding and attending karate camp."

Emma felt a horrible clutch of fear in her stomach.

Although her parents were not very nice, Emma knew that they were too stuck-up and shallow to be seriously unkind. Uncle Simon, however, was a true horror. She had met him only once, but it was enough to know that she never wanted to see him again.

Uncle Simon lived far from the city, on the edge of a town called Nummington. He was a professional hunter and owned dozens of guns. Every winter he would go on safari, returning only after he had amassed a collection of exotic heads, pelts, teeth, and claws. He then sold them to high-end buyers looking to decorate their walls with rare animals.

Two years ago, Mr. Burblee had planned a two-day visit to see him, because he wanted squirrel tails to paste on a new line of Chic-Chic hats. Mr. Burblee figured that bagging a couple of squirrels would be easy for a hunter like Uncle Simon. He had dragged Emma along because Mrs. Burblee was on a Chic-Chic model shoot in Hawaii, and the Burblees' regular babysitter had broken both her ankles and couldn't look after Emma.

Emma remembered meeting Uncle Simon for the first time on the front porch of his house. He had cold, mean eyes and soft, hairy hands. Slabs of fat rolled off his sides like blobs of melted wax oozing down a candle.

When Mr. Burblee introduced Emma, Uncle Simon turned to her and barked, "Young girl! Do you know how to make backyard stew?"

"What?"

"Backyard stew! I swear, they don't teach kids anything useful these days." Uncle Simon fixed a nasty glare on Emma. "Listen up, twerp. This is how you make the best dish in the world. What you do is nail a couple of scampering rabbits and tweeting bluebirds in the backyard. Then you churn them up in a blender. Next, you dump them in a great big pot with tripe and sheep's tongue, add a bucketful of lard, boil it awhile, then serve." Uncle Simon smacked his lips. "I make it at least twice a week for dinner. And that's what we're going to have tonight!"

Emma had spent two miserable days at Uncle Simon's as he decimated the local squirrel population, bragged about his grisly hunting exploits, and slurped down his foul stew every night at dinner. Once Mr. Burblee's suitcase was full of squirrel tails and she and her father were safely on their way back to the city, Emma had vowed never to go back.

As she looked at her mother's determined face, Emma decided that one miserable tenth birthday was worth a summer at camp, miles away from Uncle Simon.

"Okay, I'll do it," she sighed.

Mrs. Burblee clapped her pretty hands. "Wonderful! I knew you would see reason. Don't worry about the party details. I'll make sure they're perfect. Of course, we'll need nonfat, sugar-free ice cream, and I suppose we'll get a cake, but we'll make sure that it won't be full of nasty calories. And we *must* find some adorable shoes at Madame Chouchou's Shoe Emporium to go with your dress, and, yes, the candles must be custom-made Italian, and I'll order some champagne for all of the guests—of course, you won't be able to drink it, dear, but I'm sure all the adults will appreciate it—and, good heavens, we'll need our maid to clean the apartment; those bathroom gargoyles are positively *dusty* and . . ."

Emma left her babbling mother and went into her room to read. She curled up with a battered copy of her favorite cookie recipe book and tried not to think about her birthday.

✦ 5 ✦

The Birthday Party

Five days later, the dreaded Saturday arrived. An hour before the party, Emma found herself staring at the bathroom mirror. She wore a poufy red dress with sequins large enough to choke on. Her hair-sprayed curls clicked together as she moved her head. Glittery black high-heeled shoes pinched her feet, and her face was stiff with makeup.

Her mother swept in and took a look. She frowned. "Your sleeves aren't puffed enough—here, let me help."

Emma shifted uncomfortably. "They're fine. Besides, none of my friends are going to see me, since you didn't let me invite anyone."

"Your tenth birthday is too important to spend with insignificant children." Mrs. Burblee bustled over and began to plump up Emma's dress. "You will be introduced to people who could make you a *star* and give you a *career,* and you mustn't be prattling with your little buddies when the time comes. Why, the president of Bicklee's Super

Duper Toothpaste will be here, and if you smile nicely enough, he might let you be in a commercial!"

"That's right, Emma," said Mr. Burblee, striding into the bathroom. "Imagine how much money you would make if Mr. Bicklee chose *you* as his toothpaste model!"

"Dad, my teeth aren't straight," said Emma.

Mr. Burblee cringed. "Well, maybe you'll have better luck with Mrs. Finch."

"Mrs. Finch? Doesn't she sell baby diapers?" asked Emma.

There was an uncomfortable silence.

"But we must keep our options open," trilled Mrs. Burblee. "Because"—and here Mr. Burblee joined in— "YOU NEVER KNOW WHO'S GOING TO MAKE YOU RICH!"

Emma sighed and wriggled away from her mother's fussy hands. "I really don't think I'm going to impress anyone."

Mrs. Burblee patted her daughter's head. "Don't worry, dear. We'll do the impressing for you. Now run along to your room and don't come out until your father and I say so. We want to bring you out at the perfect moment."

Emma wobbled out of the bathroom on her high heels. As soon as she was out of her parents' sight, she yanked off her shoes and headed to her room.

Then she waited.

Six o'clock passed. Emma heard guests arriving, clicking

and clacking on the hard floors. High-pitched cackles and tittering laughter came in under the doorway.

She shuddered.

Seven o'clock passed. Emma was getting hungry.

No one came to get her.

Eight o'clock came around. Emma counted eighteen belly rumbles in half an hour.

By nine o'clock, she was more than ready to brave the party for a bite to eat. When nine-thirty rolled around and her parents hadn't so much as peeked into her room, Emma decided it was time to make an entrance. Gritting her teeth, she wrenched her shoes back on her feet. With one big lurch, she flung open the door . . .

. . . and bumped straight into her father as he held a gigantic cake full of flaming candles. Mr. Burblee shrieked and lost his balance. The cake tottered. It slid sideways, a six-layer, fat-free, sugar-free, chocolate-substitute monstrosity.

Emma darted forward and swooped under the cake platter as it slid out of Mr. Burblee's hands. The cake tilted upright again.

But as she moved to settle the cake on the table, the spike of her right shoe caught in a groove in the floor. She pitched forward. The cake slid slowly over her arms with a squelch and plopped to the floor. The candles sank into the frosting and sputtered out.

There was a horrific silence.

Emma stared down hungrily at the waxy brown mess.

She felt like scooping up a piece and taking a nibble, but it didn't seem like the right moment.

"What a clumsy child," drawled a voice.

Emma looked up. She saw a woman staring at her with disdain. She had dozens of gold bangles around her wrist and wore a gigantic necklace with a diamond pendant in the shape of a diaper. It was Mrs. Finch.

Emma bristled. "I am not clumsy. I would have been fine if I weren't wearing high heels."

"Any ten-year-old girl should know how to wear high heels properly," Mrs. Finch sneered. "Why, I was in four-inch heels when I was *eight.*"

"How *splendid,* Mrs. Finch!" Mrs. Burblee exclaimed hastily. "Of course, our Emma is a little slow with learning how to walk properly, but isn't she adorable? Don't you think she'd make the perfect diaper model?"

"If she can't even handle two-inch heels, how is she going to have the grace to show off my diapers?" Mrs. Finch sniffed.

Emma spoke slowly and politely. "Excuse me, Mrs. Finch, but your models don't have grace—they're babies who haven't learned to crawl yet. And high heels—or diapers, for that matter—should *not* be worn by ten-year-olds. They both give you rashes, just in different places."

"Child, you don't know what you're talking about. Rashes, indeed." Mrs. Finch turned to Mrs. Burblee. "What a grace-less, plain-looking, unspeakably ordinary child you have."

Emma burst. "I MAY BE PLAIN AND ORDINARY,

BUT AT LEAST I'M NOT A SHALLOW DIAPER-PEDDLING NINCOMPOOP LIKE YOU!" She took off a heel and flung it. It landed in the punch bowl. Red punch splattered out, and several women in white dresses shrieked.

Emma took the other shoe off and pitched it as hard as she could. It bounced off the chandelier, ricocheted off the china cabinet, then grazed past a man with the whitest teeth Emma had ever seen.

The man clutched his hand and screamed. "MY PINKY! MY BEAUTIFUL, FLAWLESS PINKY!" He uncupped his hand, and Emma saw a tiny scratch above his knuckle. The high heel lay beside him.

"Oh, no," she said.

"Emma Burblee, go to your room." Mr. Burblee's voice was dangerously high.

Emma went. She shut the door softly and stopped in front of her mirror, where she stared glumly at herself for a long, long time.

✴ 6 ✴

Nummington

Nummington was a cozy, flourishing town a seven-hour drive from the city. It lay in a valley surrounded by small green hills and patches of woods. A deep blue river wound itself along the town's outskirts, full of smooth, round river rocks and jumping pink-bellied trout. Brightly painted wooden houses lined the streets. Stores with colorful awnings and bright glass window fronts covered the center of town.

At three o'clock on a warm, sunny Sunday afternoon, a black limo rolled down the main street. Inside, Charles steered while Emma gazed out at the town. Mr. and Mrs. Burblee drank Diet Coke from champagne glasses and made snide chitchat about Uncle Simon.

"Do you remember the jacket he wore for his Christmas card picture last year?" Mr. Burblee giggled.

"How could I forget that hideous green abomination with brown polka dots?" Mrs. Burblee tipped back her bubbling drink and let off a delicate burp. "He looked like a diseased lettuce leaf."

"And probably smelled like one too." Mr. Burblee cracked open another can of fizz and drank it straight. "Still, we should get him something for letting us dump Emma on him for the summer."

"We *are* paying him a fortune to babysit her, but I suppose you're right." Mrs. Burblee thought for a moment. "What about a big, fat, sugary cake? He does love food."

"And how it shows," Mr. Burblee snickered.

Mrs. Burblee pressed a delicate hand to her mouth to stop an unpleasant snigger. She leaned over and tapped the chauffeur sharply on his shoulder. "Driver! Find us a sweet shop at once!"

"Yes, ma'am. I know just the place." Charles continued down the main street. At a stoplight, he turned and gave Emma a wink. "You're going to love it!" he whispered.

Emma gave Charles a tiny grin, then rolled down the window and peered outside. She saw a flower shop bustling with people buying daisies and tulips, a stand with carefully arranged fruit and vegetables, and a bakery with neatly braided loaves of bread laid out on large cookie trays. People walked unhurriedly from place to place and laughed and chatted with one another. Outside a storefront with chocolate and vanilla swirls on the window, small children with sticky faces happily licked ice cream cones of every flavor.

Charles slowed down and parked on the side of the street in front of a large store whose sign read: PETE'S FINE SAUSAGES AND HAMS.

7

The Cake Shop

"You dolt." Mrs. Burblee glared at Charles. "I said sweet shop, not meat shop."

"I know, ma'am." Charles looked over his shoulder. "The sweet shop is three blocks down."

"Then why are we stopping here?"

"Because this is where the line starts."

The Burblees looked down the street. Dozens and dozens of people stretched from block to block.

"Exactly what shop do you have in mind?" Mr. Burblee rumbled.

"Mr. Crackle's Cake Shop, of course. It has the best pastries in the world!" Charles beamed.

Mr. Burblee frowned. "Looks popular, but I don't want to wait in line."

"I'm sure we won't have to—after all, we *are* rich," Mrs. Burblee said airily. "Driver, keep on going until we reach the shop."

"But—"

"*Don't* argue."

Charles paused, then quietly started the limo. He drove past the long line, parked in front of the cake shop, and then got out and opened the door for the Burblees.

As Emma emerged from the limo's backseat, the gentle aroma of rich pastries filled her nostrils. She had never smelled anything so delicious in her life. She took a deep breath, stepped onto the sidewalk, and took her first look at the place with such exquisite smells.

The cake shop had a pink-and-green awning that shaded four large windows framed by green shutters. A wooden sign hung in one window, with MR. CRACKLE'S CAKE SHOP delicately etched in old-fashioned handwriting. A door with a big brass knob, well polished by countless eager hands, stood wide open.

Mrs. Burblee had gotten out of the limo. She rummaged through her purse and drew out her vial of vinegar. With a sharp sniff, she inhaled, then pressed the vial to Emma's nose.

For the first time in her life, Emma batted the vial away.

Mrs. Burblee's eyes narrowed. "Emma, take the vinegar. You don't want to be smelling all these disgust—"

"Yes, I do." Emma stared at her mom.

Mrs. Burblee flinched. Her voice turned hard and low. "Very well, young woman. You're lucky that I don't want to make a scene." She turned and began to shove past the neatly lined-up crowd at the entrance of the shop. Mr. Burblee grasped Emma's hand and followed closely.

Emma glanced at the waiting customers. "It's not very nice to cut."

"Nice, schmice. We are too important to wait behind ordinary people," Mrs. Burblee sniffed.

"Quite right, my dear," said Mr. Burblee.

They went inside.

Emma's heart fluttered. Everywhere she looked, glass display cases brimmed with the most marvelous desserts. Deep-dish apple pies with perfectly browned crusts sat snugly next to bright yellow lemon meringues and gooey chocolate cakes. White-chocolate cheesecake with raspberry swirls and strawberry jelly rolls dusted with sweetened cocoa nestled up to pear tarts glazed with maple syrup. One display case held nothing but small globes of glistening chocolate truffles.

Emma felt like she had been dropped in the middle of a miracle. She thought about the pictures in the cookbooks she had seen. They were nothing compared to the masterpieces in front of her. She turned to take one more look around. Suddenly her mother's face cut off her view.

"Emma, stop staring. You look like a fish. Now, here's how to get what you want without waiting."

Mrs. Burblee pushed forward to the head of the line.

She flashed a blinding smile at the man she had stepped in front of. "Mind if I cut?" she crooned.

The man blinked. "Actually, I do," he said, and pressed a little bell with a note card taped next to it that read CUTTER ALERT.

Instantly a boy with bright red hair and freckles appeared next to Mrs. Burblee. He looked up and said politely, "Excuse me, ma'am, but Mr. Crackle doesn't allow cutters. Please move to the back of the line."

Mrs. Burblee folded her arms. She arched one perfect eyebrow. "Little boy, do you know who I am?"

"Nope, but even the king of France isn't allowed to cut. Believe me, he tried, but Mr. Crackle gave him a talking-to and he waited in line, just like everybody else." The boy looked gravely at Mrs. Burblee, who drew herself up.

"Who's this Mr. Crackle to tell important people that they have to wait?" she huffed.

"He's the best baker in the world. He can make up any rules he wants in this shop. And if you don't go to the back, you won't get anything today." The boy stared unflinchingly at Mrs. Burblee.

Mrs. Burblee lifted her eyes and emitted an exasperated groan. "Emma," she snarled, digging into her purse and pulling out a wad of bills, "get in line and buy a cake for Uncle Simon. Your father and I will be in the limo." With a glare at the redheaded boy, she took Mr. Burblee's arm and click-clacked disapprovingly out of the shop.

Emma turned to the boy. "Sorry about that. My parents usually get what they want."

"No worries. I've handled lots of snoots like them." The boy stuck out his hand. "My name's Albie."

"I'm Emma." Emma shook his hand and smiled.

Albie beamed back. "Hey, you've got a great shake! Come on, let's get to the end of the line so you don't have to wait too long."

As they walked out of the shop, Emma asked, "So do a lot of people try to cut?"

"Yup. About twenty or so tourists try to pull the 'I'm special' trick every day. Mr. Crackle hired me to be his special cutter control person. If someone rings the bell, I walk the cutter to the back of the line to make sure they don't cut again."

"What if there are several cutters at the same time?"

Albie grinned. "The trapdoor takes care of them."

"The trapdoor?" Emma's eyes widened.

"Mmm-hmm. It's in front of the counter. If someone cuts while I'm busy, it opens up and *fffwhup!* Down goes the cutter."

"Where does the trapdoor go?"

"A very nice locked room. Once I'm done with the first cutter, I bring the second cutter up and put him in line and wait with him and that's that. It's a great system, really."

Emma and Albie reached the end of the line and got behind a plump, silver-haired woman. She had a kind face and a bright orange parasol that she held in one hand to ward off the sun. She looked at Albie and chuckled. "Another cutter, Albie?"

"Nah, Mrs. Dimple. Emma's all right." Albie pointed a finger toward the long, sullen limo across the street. "Her mom and dad were the cutters."

Mrs. Dimple clucked. "Made you get in line instead of them? Typical for spoiled parents. But don't you worry. The wait is worth it. Anything Mr. Crackle bakes is pure heaven."

Albie's eyes glittered with excitement. "They say Mr. Crackle puts all these liquids and powders and stuff in his cooking, but no one's ever seen what they are. He's got a glass window between his kitchen and the shop so you can see him bake, but no one's allowed to go past that glass. I'll bet he gets his spices straight from China."

Mrs. Dimple crouched next to Emma. "It's more than just ingredients," she said softly. "There are some people who are experts at what they do. Then there are the geniuses."

Mrs. Dimple's voice fell to a low, mysterious note. "And then . . . there are magicians—people so wondrously talented at what they do, they become more craft than person.

"Mr. Crackle is a magician. He can judge with a flick of his wrist a teaspoon or a quart without using any measuring device. When he mixes ingredients, his hands flow from the flour to the spices to the buttermilk like he's conducting a fantastic symphony. He's got magic in his fingers, magic in his blood. Anything you buy will make your taste buds sing."

Emma felt excitement blossom inside her. As they waited, she listened to Mrs. Dimple regale her with descriptions of her favorite desserts ("Marmalade scones with dobs of fresh cream—marvelous! Raspberry pistachio ice cream—heavenly!"). Before long, they had reached the front of the line.

Mrs. Dimple addressed the pleasant-faced young woman behind the counter. "Margie, my love! I'll have a blueberry pie and a box of truffles."

Margie nodded briskly. "Coming right up!" She gave Mrs. Dimple a smile. "Good choice with the truffles— I think Mr. Crackle outdid himself with this batch."

Mrs. Dimple beamed. "Get the truffles," she whispered to Emma, and gave her a friendly wink before heading out the door.

✴ 8 ✴

Uncle Simon's

𝓔mma peered down at dozens of different cakes, each more splendid than the next. "How do I choose the best chocolate one?" she mused aloud.

Margie plucked a cake from a display case and propped it on the counter. It was piled high with fluffy chocolate buttercream. She gave Emma a kind look. "Trust me, this is the best. Mr. Crackle never misses with his eight-layer chocolate cake."

Emma gasped. "*Eight* layers?"

Margie nodded. "Eight delicious parties in your mouth," she said.

Emma inhaled the buttery scent. "I'll take it! May I also have a small box of assorted truffles?"

"Of course." Margie whipped out a paper box from below the counter, neatly placed the cake inside, then bundled up the box with a bit of ribbon. She did the same with the truffles and handed them to Emma. "Enjoy!"

Emma thanked Margie and paid for the desserts. She

tucked the truffle box inside her pocket and walked back to the limo with her arms full, stopping briefly to say goodbye to Albie. Charles opened the door for her. She climbed in, where she found her parents tweezing their knuckle hairs.

"Finally. Now, off to Uncle Simon's!" Mr. Burblee ordered.

The limo slinked out of town, hit a pothole and lurched, then crept up a winding dirt road until it parked next to a ramshackle house with peeling paint and a rotting front porch.

Emma saw Uncle Simon sitting on the steps of the porch, which sagged under his enormous bulk. He was cleaning a metal-clawed trap with an oily rag.

"You're just in time for hunting rabbits!" he shouted to the Burblees as they clambered out of the limo. "Once this trap's all greased up, we're going to catch ourselves some dinner!"

"Hello, Simon. We only eat dinner every other day, but thank you for the invitation." Mrs. Burblee strode forward to greet her brother-in-law. She gave Uncle Simon air kisses while Emma and Charles collected suitcases from the trunk of the limo and hauled them up to the porch.

"Simon, nice to see you," boomed Mr. Burblee, rummaging through his pocket. He pulled out a checkbook and pen and began to scribble. When he was done, he tore off a check and handed it over.

Uncle Simon's cold eyes lit up. "Good to see we're

getting straight to business." He tucked the check in his pants and stood up. The metal trap gleamed. "So . . . I make sure Emma's still alive by the end of the summer, and in three months you come and get her and I get another one of these checks?"

"That's right!" Mrs. Burblee bobbed her head and turned to Emma. "Now, you make sure you do whatever Uncle Simon says. Once summer ends, we'll send the driver for you. Have fun!"

Mr. Burblee patted Emma's head. "See if you can find squirrel tails—the boutique is running low." He kept patting. "By the way, we left a present for you in one of your suitcases."

With that, Mr. and Mrs. Burblee turned their backs to Emma and Uncle Simon and sashayed back to the limo. Emma thanked Charles and gave him a tight hug before he left to open the door for her parents and drive away.

Uncle Simon jerked his thumb toward the door. "Your room's the one next to the kitchen. In a few hours, I'll be back with rabbit, and maybe a bluebird. The recipe for backyard stew is on the fridge. When I come back, you had better be ready to make dinner . . . or else." He gave Emma a glare, then waddled down the porch steps and disappeared into the woods.

Emma dragged her belongings into the house and found the cramped, untidy room Uncle Simon had given her. She spent the next hour dusting and sweeping, then unpacked her suitcase, in which she found a Chic-Chic hatbox. Pinned to the top was a note that read: *Dear Emma, For goodness' sake, wear this so at least some of your outfit will be fashionable. It's a Chic-Chic specialty!* Inside the box was a hat decorated with cactus prickles and pickle stems. Emma sighed and sat on her creaky bed.

It was going to be a long summer.

She pulled out her truffles and popped one into her mouth. The chocolate hesitated on her tongue, then melted into a river of sweetness. Emma closed her eyes and sighed with happiness.

Feeling much better, she decided to make a quick inspection of the house. She left her room and walked into the kitchen, a mass of stainless-steel counters and cabinets. The stove was two tons of heavy-duty iron with eight burners. Emma turned a knob and watched as monstrous blue flames leaped three inches in the air.

A steel pantry stood next to a massive walk-in fridge hunched in the corner. Emma took a peek inside and found slabs of meat, pounds of butter, cases of eggs, bags full of onions, buckets of potatoes, and assorted condiments. An enormous freezer held more slabs of meat and a few bags of frozen peas. Plates crusted over with greasy bits of left-over food filled the sink.

Emma wandered into the living room. A thick, deep couch dusted with potato-chip crumbles sat in front of a large television turned to a cooking channel. An advertisement for meat cleavers was on. To the right of the television stood an ancient grandfather clock and an enormous locked

gun cabinet with dozens of rifles and shotguns. Along the walls, just below the ceiling, were the heads of some of the poor creatures Uncle Simon had shot.

Upstairs was Uncle Simon's room, bedecked in fur rugs, greasy sandwich wrappers, and more animal heads. Dirty towels and underwear filled the bathroom next door.

The grandfather clock downstairs chimed the half hour. Emma realized she should have been preparing Uncle Simon's dinner and went down to the kitchen. She found the recipe for backyard stew, rolled up her sleeves, and began to cube potatoes. As she sliced the onions, she had a suspicion that her cooking lessons were going to come in handy.

✦ 9 ✦

Cooking and Cleaning

$\mathcal{E}$mma's suspicion proved right. As the weeks went by, Uncle Simon kept her busy with cooking and cleaning and chores. A usual day of eating would find him gobbling eight eggs and a dozen slices of bacon for breakfast, three bloody steaks and a gallon of Turkish coffee for midmorning snack, two small roasted suckling pigs for lunch, five lobsters and a broiled pheasant for afternoon snack, and seven bowls of backyard stew for dinner.

Twice a week, a great big delivery truck would arrive at the house, filled with piles of ingredients. It was all Emma could do to keep up with Uncle Simon's appetite. By the time she finished making breakfast, lunch had to be prepared, followed by chores around the house, then several hours of dinner making.

Though she was glad to finally try out her cooking skills, Emma was soon exhausted by the work she had to do for Uncle Simon, who came closest to thanking her when he wolfed down a bean-chili dinner and grunted, "Well, I'll be gassy tonight, but it was worth it."

However, there was one area of cooking that Emma did not have to worry over. Two afternoons after she arrived, Uncle Simon gave her a list that read:

3 chocolate buttercream cakes
5 blackberry jelly rolls
8 pecan pies
12 super-triple-fudge brownies
46 strawberry-rhubarb crumble squares
92 oatmeal raisin cookies
151 glazed pear tarts
289 mint truffles

"Are you having company tonight?" Emma asked.

Uncle Simon glowered down at her. "Absolutely not, you ignorant twit. This is my dessert list for the week. I normally get them delivered from Mr. Crackle's, but I never miss an opportunity to save a buck or two. Why pay extra for a pie when you have someone to make it for free?"

Emma's eyes glimmered. At last! A chance to bake dessert! She grabbed a dessert cookbook she had snuck into her suitcase and set to work.

Unfortunately, dessert baking proved harder than she thought. The egg whites didn't froth. The pastry dough turned stiff and dry. "Glaze" was much easier to say than to make.

That evening, when Emma brought out dessert, Uncle Simon took one bite and gagged.

"Pah! This tastes like burned coals!"

"I knew I should have turned down the oven." Emma looked grimly at the assorted blackened desserts on the dinner table.

Uncle Simon scowled. "I suppose I'll have to go back to Mr. Crackle. But don't think I'm going to spend any money for dessert on *you*." He stood up in disgust and stormed out.

The next afternoon, he handed Emma a wooden box he had designed to keep his desserts from getting squashed. Inside the box were walls that could slide every which way and then lock, forming compartments that would exactly fit each of the desserts. "Now listen up, you little pip-squeak," Uncle Simon barked. "You're going to get my desserts for me. You're obviously useless at baking, but at least you'll save me some cash on delivery charges."

Every few days, Emma would walk to Mr. Crackle's Cake Shop with the dessert box lashed to her back. Once she had filled it with Uncle Simon's order, she would stagger home, laden with treats she could not eat.

Upon her arrival, Uncle Simon would call out in his ugly, booming voice, "Well, Emma, I certainly hope you weren't thinking of stealing some of my dessert tonight. Because if you did, I would know. And you would not be able to sit for a week."

He would inspect every dessert, running his cruel,

piggish eyes over each scrape of frosting and each crust to make sure that Emma had not snitched a grain of sugar. Then he would sit, fingers deep in the cakes, pies, cookies, tarts, and truffles, snatching and snatching and gulping and gulping until every last bite had disappeared.

Afterward he would let loose a smelly belch, tell Emma to clean up, and waddle off to watch television. His favorite show was a reality contest called *Supreme-Extreme Master of the Kitchen,* in which chefs competed with one another for fame and fortune. Emma often wished she could watch the show—she felt as if she could have picked up some useful cooking tips. But Uncle Simon liked to heckle the cooks with blisteringly foul language, and after learning twenty-eight horrible words in one evening as she watched *Supreme-Extreme* with him, Emma decided she much preferred cleaning the kitchen when the hour-long program came on.

✳ 10 ✳

Mr. Crackle

Though Uncle Simon made life absolutely miserable, Emma soon discovered that Nummington held a world of lovely people to balance out her uncle's awfulness.

The first day she went to town with Uncle Simon's enormous dessert box on her shoulders, she felt curious glances on her as she trudged down the main street. When she passed by Pete's Fine Sausages and Ham, she bumped into Mrs. Dimple, who was just coming out of the store. In one hand she held a waxed paper package, in the other, her orange parasol. Mrs. Dimple looked at Emma and arched one eyebrow. "That's quite a box you've got there, dearie," she said.

Emma nodded. "It's for my uncle's desserts," she explained, shifting the box uncomfortably. She reached into her pocket and showed Mrs. Dimple her uncle's dessert list.

Mrs. Dimple's eyebrow inched higher. Her parasol twirled. "Are you sure you can carry all of this?"

Emma reached the end of the cake shop line and heaved the box to the ground. She shook her head. "It's a pretty heavy box, even empty. It'll take me a couple of trips to bring all of Uncle Simon's desserts back."

Mrs. Dimple stopped twirling her parasol and laid it gently against her knee. She bent down and gave the box a delicate yank. "Oomph! Pretty heavy is right! How far does your uncle live from town?"

"About a mile."

Mrs. Dimple frowned. "Tell you what. My pickup truck is parked down the street. When you've finished getting all those desserts, we'll load them up and I'll drive you home."

Emma blinked. "Are you sure, Mrs. Dimple?"

Mrs. Dimple smiled. "Absolutely."

Just then, Albie trotted up with a red-faced man in tow. "Emma! How's it going?" Albie turned to the beety man. "Now, stay in line. If you cut again, you won't get any cake."

"But . . . but I am very important!" the man sputtered. "I am the famous movie director of *Whale Bubbles* and *Popsicle Juice*! I have enough money to buy this whole town. I do *not* need to wait!" He glared at Albie.

Albie glared back.

The man sighed. "Fine," he grumbled. Crossing his arms and huffing, he stomped to the back of the line.

Satisfied, Albie turned his attention to Emma. "What's that?" he asked, pointing to the box at her feet.

Emma gave the box a little kick. "It's my uncle's dessert box. I have to load it up."

Albie gave a whistle. "You'll be stocked for weeks!"

"Nope, this will only last a few days." Emma grabbed the straps of the box and dragged it along as the line moved forward.

Mrs. Dimple gave the box a stern look. "Well, I hope he's having a large dinner party tonight!"

Emma shook her head. "It's just for him. He has a large appetite." She dragged the box another few feet.

Albie frowned. "Mr. Crackle won't like this—all those sweets for some guy who doesn't share. Here, let me talk to him for you and see what I can do." He disappeared behind the back of the cake shop.

A few minutes later, a tall, gray-haired man came out. He was wearing a blue apron spattered with cocoa. He had kind, twinkly eyes surrounded by laugh wrinkles, and he smelled of vanilla and cinnamon.

He dusted off a floury hand and offered it to Emma. "Hello, Emma. I'm Mr. Crackle. Albie tells me you've got an uncle problem."

Emma took Mr. Crackle's large, weathered hand in her own. Years of baking had made his palm rough and calloused. "Sort of. Uncle Simon feeds me enough, but he never lets me have dessert."

Mr. Crackle frowned. "I am familiar with your uncle's astronomical orders, but I did not know he ate everything himself. Do you mean to say that your uncle eats pounds and pounds of dessert a day and refuses to give you even a crumb?"

"Yup."

Mr. Crackle said thoughtfully, "What your uncle needs is a good kick in the pants."

Emma giggled.

Mr. Crackle grinned.

Albie crowed, "He sure does!"

"Now, let's see what your uncle ordered for today," Mr. Crackle said.

The wrinkled dessert list was brought forth, and desserts speedily filled Uncle Simon's box. Then the box was lifted into Mrs. Dimple's pickup, trucked to Uncle Simon's, and hustled into the kitchen. As they unpacked the desserts, Emma thanked Mrs. Dimple and Albie, who had come along to help.

"This summer is going to be much better than I thought," Emma said as she arranged truffles on a plate. "At first, all I knew was that I would have to spend all my hours with Uncle Simon. Now I'm going to try and go to town as much as I can."

"Speaking of your uncle, where is he?" Mrs. Dimple asked, sliding the chocolate buttercream cakes into the fridge.

"He's in the living room. I think he's watching a rerun of *Supreme-Extreme Master of the Kitchen*." Emma finished with the truffles and began to stack the brownies.

Albie perked up. "I love *Supreme-Extreme*! It always

has the neatest people. You know, Mr. Crackle won it, right before he set up shop in Nummington."

Mrs. Dimple nodded. "Folks say the show changes you—that winning guarantees that anything you make for the rest of your life will be an instant success."

Emma popped a truffle into her mouth that Mr. Crackle had given to her as a gift. As the sweet, rich chocolate melted on her tongue, she had to agree.

The days rolled by, and Emma grew to love Nummington. When she was not crushed by Uncle Simon's demands, she would escape to town, where she would often go over to Mrs. Dimple's house for tea and cookies. Mrs. Dimple introduced her to many of the warm, quirky townspeople, who welcomed her with jokes and stories and usually a snack or two.

If Emma was waiting in line at the cake shop, Albie would find her when he wasn't busy bringing cutters to the back of the line, and they'd chat about the best flavor of bubble gum or the right way to hold a baseball bat.

One day Emma put on her cactus-prickled, pickle-stemmed hat for her trip to Mr. Crackle's shop. When Albie saw her, he burst out laughing. He taped a bonbon to his hat, and they spent a marvelous afternoon pretending to be fancy supermodels.

Emma loved going to the cake shop every day. She loved the smells and the sights and the cheerful pink-and-green awning that hung over the shop window. She loved the gleaming and glistening pies and tarts and pastries that were lined up so neatly in the enormous glass display case.

But most of all, she loved the kindness of the cake shop's owner. Mr. Crackle made sure that anytime Emma wanted a pastry, she could help herself. And every once in a while, if Emma came in with an especially frustrated face because Uncle Simon was being particularly horrid, Mr. Crackle would doctor a dessert with something that caused uncontrollable itching or knuckle cramps.

And so Emma might have spent the entire summer avoiding her uncle and having a lovely time in Nummington but for a knock at the door two months after her fluff-headed parents plopped her down on her uncle's front porch.

✳ 11 ✳

The Visitor

One evening when Emma was scrubbing the toilet with a toothbrush (Uncle Simon spent lavishly on food, not cleaning supplies), she heard a rapping at the door.

Tap tap. Tap tap. Tap tap.

"Uncle Simon, someone's at the door!" Emma called.

"Answer it, brat, and if it's not my steak delivery, throw them out!" yelled Uncle Simon from the upstairs bedroom.

Emma sighed, wiped her hands, and went to the door.

Before she could turn the knob, it twisted on its own and the door swung open. A man stepped into the room.

He was dressed in a white suit that was impeccably ironed. He had white gloves, a white hat, and a white cane. He was bony and tall, and his eyes had a glint to them that made Emma shudder.

"Where is Simon Burblee?" the man asked in a cold, thin voice.

"He's upstairs. Are you a new steak deliveryman?" asked Emma.

The man gave Emma a withering look. "Child, do not ask stupid questions." He swept past Emma and called out, "Simon Burblee, show yourself this instant!"

Heaving and thumping were heard upstairs, and the weighty bulk of Emma's uncle came waddling down the stairs. In his left hand he carried an enormous piece of chocolate cake, while his right hand gripped a giant mug of milk. He swigged the milk and latched his jaws onto the cake. He caught sight of the visitor and stopped.

A twisted look of delight came over his face. "Why, if it isn't Maximus Beedy! I haven't seen you since we shot tree sloths on our hunting trip three years ago! How are you? And what are you doing here? I thought you were in Tuptiddy City extracting scorpion poison for the School of Assassins!"

"I was, until I found something I couldn't pass up. Wait until you hear what I've discovered," said Maximus Beedy.

Uncle Simon looked at Emma. "Get back to work, you detestable slug. I don't want a speck of grime on my toilet seat." With that, he and Maximus Beedy disappeared into the living room.

Emma hesitated, then tiptoed over to peer through the keyhole.

". . . the time when you shot that baby zebra? I thought I would die laughing," Uncle Simon chortled.

"Good times," Maximus Beedy said curtly. "But even

better times are ahead of us if you just shut your mouth for a moment and listen to what I have to say."

Uncle Simon stopped laughing abruptly. "Go on," he said, his voice dripping with greed.

Maximus Beedy perched fastidiously on the edge of the couch. "I was in the catacombs underneath Tuptiddy City hunting for scorpions," he began. "But there was another reason why the catacombs interested me so much. They hold the skeletons of famous rulers, including Emperor Fuddlykoo of the twelfth century."

Uncle Simon gulped down his milk and burped. "Fuddlykoo? Wasn't he the one who kept offing his chefs?"

"The very one." Maximus rubbed the top of his cane. "Fuddlykoo had a fickle sense of taste coupled with a bad temper, and most cooks didn't last long in his kitchen. One day he would gobble up pickled spiders' toes, and the next day he couldn't stand them. On Monday he'd stuff himself stupid with roasted pheasant eggs, while on Tuesday the smell of them sent him into convulsions. No one is sure why. I suppose he was picky."

"Extremely picky," snorted Uncle Simon. He thrust a blobby hand into his pocket and pulled out a lint-covered licorice stick. "Candy, Maximus?"

Maximus shuddered. "No."

"Suit yourself." Uncle Simon gnawed at the licorice, lint and all.

Maximus pursed his lips, then continued. "Fuddlykoo lopped off six hundred and twenty-nine heads before he hired a pastry chef named Alexus Mastivigus. Mastivigus was the most talented baker in the world, but that wasn't what kept his head off the chopping block. He had supposedly created an elixir that would make any food taste irresistibly delicious. When Fuddlykoo died, Mastivigus buried the elixir recipe with him. Since I was already going to the catacombs underneath Tuptiddy City on business, I went to investigate. I found this hidden among Fuddlykoo's remains."

Through the keyhole, Emma saw Maximus reach into his coat pocket and remove a scroll made of ancient, yellowed parchment. He handed it to Uncle Simon.

There was a silence. Then Emma heard Uncle Simon say, "Maximus, this is a recipe for your mother's chicken casserole."

"Sorry, wrong one." Maximus dug back into his pocket and pulled out another scroll. He handed it to Simon.

After several moments, Emma heard her uncle's voice. "Bah. I can't understand any of this. And, anyway, it won't work. Nothing in the world can make any kind of food instantly delicious."

"Aha! I thought so too. But just to be sure, I sent the recipe to some very talented bakers, promising them fame and fortune if they made the recipe correctly. All but Maddie Tinkleberry failed."

"Maddie Tinkleberry? *The* Maddie Tinkleberry? The winner of last year's Supreme-Extreme Master of the Kitchen Contest?"

"The very one," replied Maximus Beedy. "She managed to get it precisely right. I meant to dispose of her afterward so she would never be able to make the potion again—after all, you can't have gallons and gallons of this stuff around or it becomes worthless—but a day after she gave me the potion, she disappeared." Maximus looked down and swung his cane in a slow circle. "I searched the world for her for eight months, but she never turned up. Then I realized that she probably knew I was hunting for her. If she replicated the elixir and tried to sell it, I'd immediately pinpoint her whereabouts. And if she has to lie low for the rest of her life, then the elixir and the money it can make is all mine!"

Through the keyhole, Emma saw Maximus Beedy take a small glass bottle from his coat. It couldn't have held more than a teaspoonful.

"Behold the Elixir of Delight, the most valuable liquid in the world!" crowed Maximus. "With it, you will charm the taste buds of anyone you please. One drop will adapt to suit the taste of every man, woman, and child."

"You don't mean . . ."

"Ah, yes, but I do. You can put a drop in a pile of sawdust and people will knock each other over to eat it."

"Which means they'll be willing to pay for it . . ." Uncle Simon's eyes glimmered.

"Yes, Simon, yes! You catch my drift! It is very simple. We set up a cake shop in this town, throw together flour, water, and food coloring so it looks something like cake,

add a drop of elixir, and presto! You can charge any price—anything you want—and people will pay. It will taste like heaven to them, only better."

"But that bottle doesn't hold enough to spit in—"

"We don't need much to get rich. This bottle is good for two hundred servings. We'll charge a horrendous price and bankrupt this rich old town, then head south for the rest of our lives!"

Uncle Simon's voice suddenly turned suspicious. "Maximus, you are my best friend, but you do have a reputation for being horribly greedy. Why are you letting me in on this scheme?"

"My dear Simon, if I told you it was out of the goodness of my heart, I would be lying, and you would know it," Maximus said. "So here's the real reason. I need someone respectable enough to run a pastry shop. Of all my friends, you are the only one who is not in jail, on the run, or trying to conquer Greenland. If you're up for it, we'll buy a shop tomorrow, and within the month we'll be millionaires!"

Emma heard her uncle's triumphant drawl. "What a splendid plan. Of course I'm up for it. I've been hoping to rid myself of my maggot of a niece without losing the money her parents pay me to babysit her. With this elixir, I'll get rich and throw her out! Hooray! No more nasty kid on my hands! Whoopee!"

It was at times like this that Emma hated her uncle most.

"Simon, we'll need a safe place to keep the elixir and the recipe."

"I have just the spot. Bring them over to my gun cabinet. I'll store them between the A-Bolt Stainless Stalker and the Savage 10GXP3."

"Simon, you and I are going to cheat the pants off this town and get rich, rich, rich!"

As the two men cackled, Emma quietly retreated from the keyhole and tiptoed up the stairs.

✦✷ 12 ✷✦

A Soapy Idea

$\mathcal{E}$mma returned to the bathroom and scrubbed furiously with the toothbrush as she thought. She came to three conclusions:

1. Maximus Beedy was not the new steak deliveryman.
2. If Maximus and her uncle succeeded with their plan, their pastry shop would drive Mr. Crackle out of business.
3. She had to stop them.

If only I could make one of them drop the elixir bottle and smash it to bits, she thought. *Then they'd have to make the recipe all over again, and it sounds like no one can do that.*

Finished with the toilet, she threw the toothbrush into the trash and walked to the sink. She turned on the water and began to lather her hands with a bar of soap. Suddenly the soap slipped out of her hands. She tried to grab it before it fell, but the bar slid past her fingers and dropped to the floor. As it hit, it broke in two.

As Emma picked up the pieces, an idea occurred to her.

Soap!

Slick soap!

Coat the bottle with soap and whoever picks it up will be sure to drop it!

Excitedly, Emma rinsed off her hands and charged into her room to form her plan.

✳ 13 ✳

The Plan Unfolds

That night, after Uncle Simon and Maximus had gone to bed, Emma slipped on her pajamas, then quietly opened her closet door and pulled out a metal hanger.

She unraveled the thin line of steel that coiled around itself to form the hook and smoothed out the bends, making a long, straight wire. Using a rubber band, she attached a small piece of cloth to one end.

Then she sat down and waited.

Midnight passed. Emma didn't move.

At one o'clock, she was still sitting.

Two o'clock passed. Outside, the wind blew softly.

At three o'clock, when even the owls had flown back to their trees and settled in for the night, Emma finally stirred. She gently picked up the hanger and silently crossed the room. She twisted the doorknob and, inch by inch, pulled the door open.

Barefoot, she treaded softly down the hallway and into the kitchen. Moonlight glimmered through a window above the sink. She could see the dish-soap bottle resting near the faucet. She gathered up the soap and headed to the living room.

She was about to open the door when she heard something shift on the other side of it.

Emma pressed her eye to the keyhole and saw Maximus Beedy lying stiff-straight on the living room couch, arms crossed, like a slumbering vampire.

Well, Emma thought. *This will be interesting.* She took a deep breath, steadied her trembling hands, then cracked open the door.

Maximus didn't move.

Emma moved slowly toward the gun cabinet, fixing her eyes on the sleeping figure, looking for any sign of waking. There was none.

After several minutes, Emma reached the cabinet. It was tall and wide and wooden, with four glass doors. Inside were the stacks of guns her uncle owned. The weapons gleamed black in the pale cabinet light.

Emma crouched and scanned the bottom ledge of the cabinet. She spotted the bottle immediately, tucked between two large rifles. It was some two feet below the keyhole of the leftmost door.

Emma opened the soap bottle and dipped into it the piece of cloth attached to the hanger. She pushed the cloth through the keyhole and fed the wire through, until the cloth just touched the top of the bottle. With patient, delicate strokes, she moved the wire so the soapy cloth brushed each side of the bottle, creating a layer of invisible slipperiness. She then pulled the wire until the cloth slipped back through the keyhole.

She had done it! Whoever picked up that bottle would be sure to break it! Emma grinned and turned to go.

Her grin vanished.

Someone was turning the doorknob.

14

Discovered

Emma dove behind the couch and ducked her head down just as the door swung open. Heavy steps moved toward the cabinet. It was Uncle Simon.

He glanced at the snoring Maximus Beedy, and his mouth curled into a nasty smile. He shuffled over to the gun cabinet, riffled through his pocket, and pulled out a key. There was a soft click as he turned the key in the lock and opened the door.

In the glow of the cabinet light, Emma saw her uncle bend over and close his fingers around the bottle. He stood up and let out a small chuckle.

As he turned to go, the bottle slipped from his hand.

With a gigantic *CRACK!* it hit the floor and broke.

Maximus Beedy's eyes flew open. His thin fingers leaped to a lamp switch and pressed it on. He looked at Simon, then at the liquid disappearing into the cracks of the floor.

"SIMON BURBLEE, WHAT HAVE YOU DONE?!" he screamed.

Uncle Simon looked at his hand, then at the shattered pieces of the bottle, then at Maximus Beedy. He gurgled and sputtered, but no words came out.

"You miserable, double-crossing, unscrupulous TRAITOR!" shrieked Beedy. "You were taking the bottle for yourself, weren't you?! I ought to hang you by your toes above a crocodile-infested swamp! How *dare* you try to steal from me? And look what you've done! The Elixir of Delight is gone! You . . ."

Emma plugged her ears and shut her eyes for good measure. She was certain she wasn't supposed to know the words coming out of Maximus Beedy's mouth.

A few minutes passed. The muffled sounds and shouts abruptly stopped.

Emma suddenly remembered she had dropped the wire and soap in front of the gun cabinet.

She opened her eyes. She saw a pair of brown slippers. She saw a pair of bare feet. She braced herself.

"YOU BACKSTABBING SLUG!" roared Uncle Simon. He stooped over and wrapped his stubby fingers around Emma's arm, yanking her to her feet. In his other hand were the wire hanger and the dish soap.

On the floor sat Maximus Beedy, his face ashen as he stared at the glittering pieces of the bottle.

"YOU OVERHEARD OUR PLAN AND YOU MADE ME DROP THE ELIXIR!" Uncle Simon screamed.

Emma glared at her uncle. "Yes, I did, you horrible, horrible man! You can't cheat the entire town of Nummington! And what about Mr. Crackle? You'd run him out of business, and then where would you get all your desserts to stuff your horrible face with?"

"You wretched brat! If the townsfolk are stupid enough to eat flavored sawdust, then they deserve to be cheated! As for Mr. Crackle, I was going to hire him as my personal dessert baker."

"He would never do that! He knows what a monster you are."

"Who is Mr. Crackle?" asked Maximus Beedy.

"He owns a cake shop in Nummington. I get my desserts from him," replied Uncle Simon.

"Mr. Crackle is the best baker in the world. I bet his desserts could beat out your stupid elixir any day!" Emma yelled.

"Is that so?" Maximus Beedy said. "I've heard of this Mr. Crackle, but I figured he was too old and decrepit to be good anymore." He slowly rubbed the top of his cane. "Simon, put your niece somewhere she can't escape. We're going to have a talk."

✴ 15 ✴

To the Cake Shop

Emma wrapped her arms around her legs and shivered in the walk-in fridge, which Uncle Simon had padlocked from the outside. Despite the cold, she was fuming. Her uncle was even more detestable than she had thought. *He's so greedy he'd even cheat his best friend! And now he knows I made the bottle slip. This isn't going to be a pleasant morning.*

A moment later, Uncle Simon reappeared. He pointed at Emma. "You. Get dressed and be on the porch in five minutes."

Five minutes later, Uncle Simon, Maximus Beedy, and Emma were in Uncle Simon's car, headed toward Mr. Crackle's Cake Shop. As they wound up the main street, they spotted a light shining from the back of the shop.

Uncle Simon parked the car, jerked Emma out, and wobbled around the corner to the back entrance. Maximus followed closely.

With one large, meaty fist, Uncle Simon pounded on the door. "Crackle! Open up!"

The door opened. Mr. Crackle stood looking at the three figures with a puzzled smile. "Why, hello, Emma! And your uncle, I presume? And by the looks of it, your uncle's friend? How fortunate. I've just taken a batch of cookies out of the oven, and I need people to taste them. I'm afraid I don't let people in my kitchen, but come around to the front and I'll get you fixed right up."

"Crackle, we're not here to eat your flipping cook—" began Uncle Simon, but he stopped as they were all hit by the most exquisite smell.

It was the smell of pumpkin and cinnamon, toasted walnuts, dark, rich spices, and pure vanilla. It curled and danced in their nostrils, a heady, thick aroma of freshly baked goodness.

Maximus Beedy tapped his cane gently on the back door. "Mr. Crackle, I suggest you let us into your kitchen. We have some important matters to discuss with you. And if you don't, I'm afraid you will be putting little Emma in grave danger."

Maximus stared at Mr. Crackle.

His eyes were dangerous, glittering.

Mr. Crackle frowned. "Come in." He stepped back as Maximus, Uncle Simon, and Emma entered the kitchen.

Emma saw a long, rectangular room with brightly painted yellow walls. An enormous counter lined one side, while on the other side stood a mixer large enough to hold ten gallons' worth of batter, two ovens, five cooling racks, a refrigerator, and a dishwasher. A tall spice cabinet filled with hundreds of spices in clear bottles stood at the back of the kitchen next to barrels labeled FLOUR, SUGAR, CHOCOLATE CHUNKS, CRUSHED PEPPERMINT, ALMONDS, and RAISINS. Pots and pans and cups and whisks and stirring spoons and zesters and peelers and ladles and strainers hung from hooks dangling from the ceiling.

It was the most cheerful, well-stocked kitchen Emma had ever seen.

Mr. Crackle picked up a spatula and slid it neatly underneath three cookies. He handed one to each of his visitors. "There may be a bit too much cinnamon in them, but tell me honestly, what do you think?"

Emma, Uncle Simon, and Maximus each took a bite.

They chewed. They swallowed. They smiled.

Emma smiled because she had never tasted a better cookie.

Uncle Simon and Maximus Beedy smiled for a very different reason.

"Simon, I think we've found what we're looking for," said Maximus.

"Well, it is unusual for customers to come looking for pumpkin walnut cookies at four in the morning, but I suppose some people in the world have to be strange," said Mr. Crackle.

Maximus's smile grew wider and uglier. "We weren't looking for cookies. We were looking for someone who can make us a special recipe, a recipe that is only possible for the exceptionally talented baker. You are exceptionally talented. You will make it for us."

"Aha. And if I'm too busy?"

Maximus twitched his eyebrows. "I do not think you will be too busy, Mr. Crackle. Let me introduce myself. My name is Maximus Beedy. I am a professional poisoner."

"Well, that's very impressive, Maximus. My name is Gregor Crackle. I'm a professional baker, which I daresay is more respectable, though certainly less glamorous, than a poisoner." Mr. Crackle dug his spatula under two more cookies and began to pile them onto a plate. "Tell me, is it true that nightshade kills more quickly when mixed with strawberry juice, or was one of my friends just pulling my leg?"

"I do not think you take me seriously, Mr. Crackle," hissed Maximus. He put his hand into his pocket and with a jerk pulled it out. Emma saw the glint of a silver ring on his thumb. The bottom of the ring was curved into a needle-sharp point.

As quick as lightning, Maximus grasped Mr. Crackle's hand. Mr. Crackle flinched and cocked his head at Maximus. "You're a bit strange," he said.

Maximus pulled back his hand. There was a small red mark where the ring had touched Mr. Crackle's palm.

Maximus's lips curled into an ugly, awful smile. "Mr. Crackle, I have just pricked you with a rather nasty poison made from the sap of the joobajooba plant. Distilled eighty-seven times and combined with nightshade and powdered wolf fangs, it has a most curious power. Every few hours, you will lose one of your senses—first smell, then taste, touch, hearing, and sight. In thirty-six hours, your world will be utterly gone."

"MONSTER!" Emma hurled herself at Maximus, only to have Uncle Simon's blubbery hand yank her back. "YOU RAT! YOU NO GOOD, SKUNK-SMELLING, HORRIBLE, FILTHY—"

"Emma, don't worry. It'll be all right," Mr. Crackle said. He turned to Maximus and regarded him with an arched eyebrow. "Hmm. Joobajooba poison, did you say?"

Maximus stamped his cane. He looked exasperated. "Yes, joobajooba poison. Now, I suggest you make the recipe, and quickly. Succeed, and I will give you the antidote to the poison. Fail, and Nummington will no longer have its prize baker."

"*Harrumph.* You are quite a distasteful fellow. Let me see the recipe." Mr. Crackle took the parchment scroll from Maximus and ran his eyes over the spidery writing. Emma glowered at Maximus and kicked at Uncle Simon's shins, trying to break free until he bellowed, "EMMA BURBLEE, IF YOU KICK ME ONE MORE TIME, I WILL TAKE MAXIMUS'S RING AND STAB YOU MYSELF!"

"Shhh, be quiet!" Mr. Crackle frowned at Uncle Simon, then went back to the parchment. "Hmm. Mmm-hmm. Must check the cupboards for burberry beans . . . I'll need my special strainer for the timtam tea. . . . Oh, that's difficult.

Hmm." Mr. Crackle looked up and leveled his gaze on Maximus. "Well, I can do this, but I'll need an assistant." He turned to Emma. "Emma, how would you like to do some baking for the next few hours?"

"Sure, Mr. Crackle. But tell my uncle to let me go!"

Mr. Crackle beamed. "Wonderful. Mr. Burblee, kindly release Emma. Emma, don't kick your uncle. Now, gentlemen, I have some work to do. Come back at ten minutes before noon tomorrow and I'll have your recipe prepared. It should be just in time, right before I lose my sight. Be warned—if you come later, I don't believe I can help you. Thank you for trying my pumpkin walnut cookies."

Mr. Crackle ushered the two men out. He turned to Emma, who stared at him, aghast. "Mr. Crackle! How can you be so calm when you've been poisoned?!"

Mr. Crackle chuckled. "Emma, don't worry. The recipe for the Elixir of Delight is tricky but certainly manageable."

"But what if the recipe takes more than a day to make? What if you don't have all the ingredients? What if—"

"Emma, I will be perfectly fine," Mr. Crackle said firmly. He rerolled the parchment and tied it with string, then turned to her. "Well, it's far too early in the morning for you to be up. You should get some sleep. Follow me."

He walked briskly to the back of the kitchen and opened a heavy oak door that led to a tiny spiral staircase. Emma climbed the steps after him and found herself in a cozy attic room. She suddenly felt very tired. Morning sun was creeping through the windows and the skylight in the slanted ceiling, softly illuminating a bookcase filled with ancient-looking tomes bound in leather. Emma sleepily glanced at a few of the titles—*The Basics of Cake, Meringue Magic, Pies Pies Pies!, Chef Toutou's Baking Home Companion, Culinary Practical Jokes.* Next to the bookcase, a small, old-fashioned typewriter perched on a wooden desk studded with small drawers. A small table with two chairs sat in front of a tall window. A bed lay at the far end of the room, opposite a purple couch with orange flowers.

Mr. Crackle rummaged through his closet and pulled out a thick blanket and a pillow. "Here you go, Emma. The couch is hideous, I know, but it's extremely comfortable. I need to go back to baking, but I'll wake you in a few hours and we'll go shopping for ingredients. It's been a while since I've gone down the flour barrel."

Emma wanted to ask Mr. Crackle what he meant, but she was too sleepy to do anything but yawn. She curled up on the flowered couch and in a moment was fast asleep.

✴ 16 ✴

Morning

Emma woke to the smell of burning. She opened her eyes groggily, then snapped awake as the odor of charred sugar grazed her nose. She pulled on her shoes and hurried downstairs.

Mr. Crackle was standing over the counter with a blowtorch. He wore pink protective goggles and green flame-resistant gloves. He whistled happily as he aimed the torch at several dozen custard cups spread out on the counter. Once he had finished flaming them, he set down the torch and turned to Emma.

"Why, hello, Emma! Care for some crème brûlée?"

"No thanks, Mr. Crackle. But if you don't mind, could I have something to eat?"

"Of course!" Mr. Crackle removed his goggles and gloves. "Sorry about the smell—it's an unfortunate sensation one must experience when making brûlée. Though, to tell you the truth, that poison of Mr. Beedy's is working remarkably well—I can't smell a thing. Anyway, why don't I whip up some peanut butter and jam sandwiches while you get us some milk? Cups are in the cupboard behind you."

As Emma hopped onto the counter to reach the cups, she heard a knocking on the glass separating the kitchen from the front of the shop. She looked over and saw Albie, with a surprised face, tapping away.

"Mr. Crackle, Albie's here!" she called.

"Oh, good, we need him too. I always thought that freckly young man could be put to better use than just cutter control," Mr. Crackle called back. "Pop around to the front and bring him back here. Today we have more important things at hand than selling cake. I'll tell Margie to close up shop for a few days after she sells what I baked this morning."

Emma ran out the back door and around the shop to the front. "Hey, Albie," she panted.

"Emma! How did you get into the kitchen with Mr. Crackle? I've never seen him let anybody else in there while he's mixing things up!"

Emma took a few moments to explain to Albie what had happened. When she finished, he scratched his head. "So . . . you're saying that one of your uncle's friends poisoned Mr. Crackle, and you've got to make a special potion or else Mr. Crackle is toast?"

Emma nodded. "Yup. Will you help him? Oh, please say you will!"

Albie snorted. "Will I help? Is the ocean wavy? Of course!"

Emma gave Albie a tight hug, and they raced back to the kitchen, where Mr. Crackle was putting the finishing touches on some exquisite-looking peanut butter and jam sandwiches. Once he was done, they carried their meal upstairs to eat.

As they sat at the table munching, Emma hesitantly said, "Mr. Crackle? Can I ask you a few questions?"

"Why, certainly, Emma. What's on your mind?"

"Well, you're not scared of being poisoned, and I'm not sure why. Most people I know would be screaming or fainting every three minutes or throwing a tantrum or *something.* And then you seemed so calm and sure when Mr. Beedy asked if you could make the recipe. I can't help thinking you don't need my help. And then I thought I heard something about going down a flour barrel to go shopping, but I wasn't sure what you meant. I was pretty tired, and I think I might have heard wrong . . . but are we going down a flour barrel to go shopping?" Emma paused to catch her breath.

Mr. Crackle tapped his nose thoughtfully. "Emma, the answer to your first question is easy. I'm not scared because I trust my skills enough to make the elixir correctly. As for your other questions, I'm going to answer them by telling you a story. Many bits of the story you have to promise me you won't tell a soul. That goes for you too, Albie. What I'm about to say is extremely secret. Can you do that?"

"Of course," Emma chimed.

"Sure thing, Mr. Crackle!" Albie said.

"Well, then," said Mr. Crackle. "Here we go." He settled back in his chair.

✳ 17 ✳

Mr. Crackle's Story

"I knew when I was very small that I wanted to bake," began Mr. Crackle. "My mother was an extraordinary cook who owned a cake shop, much like mine. 'Gregor,' she told me, 'there are a few things you must know to be a baker. One, you must learn the secret to every ingredient and spice. You must learn their taste, their texture, their color, their essence. You must learn what they are like alone, in pairs, in medleys, in orchestras! You must also learn to make recipes perfectly. There are plenty of people who are and were magnificent bakers, and should you stumble across a recipe of theirs, you must be able to imitate it flawlessly. This will make you a good baker. What makes you a *great* baker is your imagination. You must be able to hunt for perfect flavors, combining the exact ingredients in the exact amount in the exact order to make exactly what you want. You must be daring and adventurous and brave and courageous!'" Mr. Crackle smiled. "Mother was a wordy person, but she loved her pastries."

"She sounds lovely," said Albie. "Please go on."

"I inherited my mother's love of making sweets, so when I grew up, I went to the Culinary Arts School in Athens to become a pastry chef," continued Mr. Crackle. "While there, I participated in the most prestigious competition a baker can enter—the annual Supreme-Extreme Master of the Kitchen Contest. It is over one thousand years old, and the winner is declared the most talented chef in the world."

Emma polished off her last bite of sandwich. "Albie told me you won the Supreme-Extreme contest before moving to Nummington." She frowned. "Why does it have such a funny name?"

Mr. Crackle sighed and rose to clear the table. "It used to be called the *Grand Prix du Gâteau,* but fifty years ago there was a very close match between François Dupin from France and Hank Smith from America. Hank won. François was a powerful man, and he was so miffed over losing that he got the French government to forbid the competition to be named in French. Hank was given the honor of renaming the competition. 'Supreme-Extreme Master of the Kitchen' was what he chose."

Cups and plates in hand, Mr. Crackle walked to the sink and turned on the water. "Apparently it was a great name for publicity. The competition used to be known to only a handful of experts who dedicated their lives to the culinary arts, but about ten years ago, a television producer caught wind of it. A year later, *Supreme-Extreme Master of the Kitchen* went on the air. I'm afraid it's now more about pizzazz and showmanship instead of the art of good cooking, but it's still a grand way of finding talented master chefs." He began to soap and rinse the dishes.

"Anyway," he went on, "many years ago, well before the Supreme-Extreme was put on television, I entered the competition and won. I got a sizable chunk of money, but after the hoopla was done and everyone went home, I was pulled aside by the judges, all previous Supreme-Extreme winners. They showed me the true prize of the contest."

"And what was it?" asked Emma.

Mr. Crackle beamed. "A key to a door that opens into a most marvelous shop! Inside the shop are jars filled with spice combinations unlike any flavors you have ever tasted! Each bottle is created from the combined knowledge of all past great bakers who discovered the most exquisite blends of flavors."

By now Mr. Crackle had stopped washing dishes and was dancing. He continued, "Take pumpkin pie spice, for example. It is a precise proportion of cinnamon, nutmeg, ginger, and allspice that does wonders for bland pumpkin. Now think of jars upon jars upon jars of spice combinations that make cookies burst with flavor, pies and tarts sweet and delectable; then think of the creative chef who combines these spice combinations and—voilà!—you have incredibly complex and beautiful flavorings unmatched by anyone except those with access to this shop."

"Sounds marvelous!" Albie got up and started to jig along with Mr. Crackle. Emma laughed and joined them.

"And that's only half of it!" Mr. Crackle said. "The other half of the shop is filled with the rarest ingredients in the world, found in places as deep as magma beds located thousands of miles underground or as far up as outer space! One of my favorite ingredients is moon sugar. I put it in my chocolate truffles for just the right sweetness."

Emma stopped dancing. A worm of a thought had just occurred to her. "This is very interesting, Mr. Crackle, but you don't have much time to make the elixir. What does the spice shop have to do with the recipe we need to make?" she asked. "And why do we have to go down the flour barrel?"

"Ah, there's a reason why I knew you'd be an excellent assistant, Emma! Sometimes I do get carried away when it comes to baking. It's good for you to remind me that we have a task at hand."

Mr. Crackle stopped dancing and lowered his voice. "Most of the ingredients in the recipe are found only at the spice shop. And the flour barrel is how I get there. Every Supreme-Extreme Master has a portal installed in his or her kitchen. I'm not sure about the physics of it, but one day a few men came into my kitchen, fiddled with the flour barrel, and now there's a little ladder that leads down to a door. I open it with a little key, and—ta-da!—I'm in the shop!"

"But, Mr. Crackle, why do you need us for this recipe?"

Emma asked. "It sounds like you can get the ingredients and stuff for yourself!"

"Frumping fiddlesticks! I forgot. You two haven't seen the recipe yet." Mr. Crackle went over to the bookshelf where the recipe lay curled up. He unrolled the parchment and smoothed it out on the table.

"Take a look," he said.

✳18✳

The Recipe

$\mathcal{E}$mma and Albie craned their necks to read the writing. Here is what they saw:

ELIXIR OF DELIGHT
Created by Alexus Mastivigus for
His Lord Highness Emperor Fuddlykoo
Makes anything taste delicious
Servings: 200

Squoil 2 burberry beans
A curled-up squid, 5 guzzle spleens
Masher 10 whingbuzzit legs
A sack of sogs, 3 biddle hegs
Frizzle the mizzle of a jug-jug tree
Skizzle the spizzle of a shick shack shree
Clunch and glunch and sklunch and zunch
10 tooby tibs of timtam tea
Squinch a wibbly cobbyseed

Splinch a skibbly hoppy mead
Add a splash of juice, then dash
A flib of fribs into the stash
Crix the bits and scrips together
Then go outside and check the weather
If it's raining, catch six drops
Add them to six gobs of trops
In sunny weather, catch a ray
And shine it in three bloobs of blay
Mirp and moil, krisk and kroil
Return to heat and let it boil
Then add the gloamy foamy ball
Of a chixed-up, fixed-up spider shawl
Slommer till the liquid's brown
Cool until the temp goes down
2.6.3 degrees
(Make sure the middle does not freeze)
Plat into a spiky hat
Twill three times, then quickly splat
The mixture through a tickler's thread
(One dyed bricky bracky red)
Finally—and this is key—
Add lifflets from the Timtim Sea
Until the buds of mobbly molds
Turn glowing glinting haunting golds
Then you'll know you've got it right
You've made the Elixir of Delight
Well done! Hooray! Yippee! Yip-yay!

Put on your happy pants today!
But, oh, beware the witchy hour
When potent powers turn sickle sour
Good shall turn from bad to worse
For those that taste at Creeker's curse.

Emma and Albie looked up. Mr. Crackle was beaming at them. "You see? You two are crucial to the creation of this elixir! You are the mobbly molds!"

Albie puzzled his eyebrows. "Mr. Crackle, what's a mobbly mold? And how do you squoil a squid? Or do any of these things in this recipe? It's all a bunch of made-up verbs and nouns that don't make sense!"

Mr. Crackle frowned. "Oh dear, I keep forgetting that most people don't know chef-speak. After spending my entire life using both ordinary and obscure cooking terms, I don't remember what is and isn't common English. Here, let me show you something."

He went to the bookshelf and removed an enormous volume with a wrinkled leather cover. He placed it on the table in front of Emma and Albie. On the front, in gold spidery lettering, was *The Encyclopedia of Eccentric Baking Terms.*

"This book contains rare cooking definitions that have fallen out of practice in the last few hundred years. Take a look at this entry." Mr. Crackle riffled through the crackly yellowed pages and found the one he wanted.

mobbly mold (n) \maw-blee mohld

(AD 98–187) Mobbly Mold was a doctor and scientist who discovered why children often change their minds about what they like to eat.

The tongue has millions of taste buds. Each bud tastes one of four distinct flavors: sweet, sour, salty, and bitter. Mobbly Mold found that in children, these buds cluster around the exact center of the tongue in an area no bigger than a grain of sugar. This area is called the taste explosion center. See diagram below:

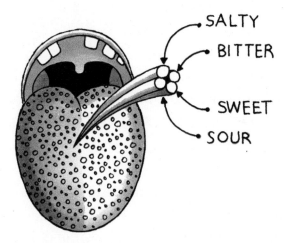

Space is tight, so the different buds battle one another to control the child's sense of taste. One day the sweet buds might win and the child will eat sugar uncontrollably. Another day the bitter buds triumph, and a child might eat almond skins like mad.

On a child's eleventh birthday, the taste explosion center explodes and the buds migrate over the tongue—sweet buds go to the tip, sours head back near the tonsils, salties stay in the middle, and bitters settle on the sides.

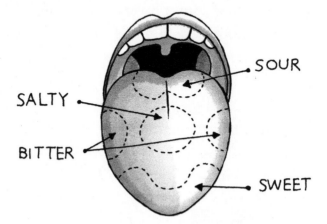

At this point, the buds have enough room so they stop bickering with one another, and the eleven-year-old begins to develop tastes that will last a lifetime.

In very rare cases, the taste explosion center does not explode and a person cannot, for the rest of his life, make up his mind what in diddly-squat he actually likes. This is called *tasteritis,* the most famous case being that of Emperor Fuddlykoo of Tuptiddy City.

A child under eleven whose taste explosion center has not exploded is referred to as a "mobbly mold" in chef-speak.

✦ 19 ✦

Getting Ready

"Huh," mused Emma. "So that explains why I keep changing my mind about creamed spinach."

Albie wrinkled his nose. "Creamed spinach—ugh! It's always horrible. Creamed mushrooms, though—I never know if I'm going to like them from one day to the next."

Mr. Crackle closed the book and returned it to the shelf. "As you see, both of you have an enormous role in the creation of the Elixir of Delight. Each of you is a mobbly mold while your taste explosion center is still intact. Since the elixir recipe says 'mobbly molds'—as in more than one—I'm assuming that I need at least two children under eleven to try out this potion, and I figured you two would do just fine. Once we get the potion right, the exact center of your tongue should turn a beautiful, sparkling gold. Now, I think it's time we got started. Let's pop downstairs and figure out what ingredients we need."

Mr. Crackle went to his desk and opened a drawer. After plucking out a sheet of paper and a pen, he motioned for Emma and Albie to follow him to the kitchen.

Back downstairs, he gave Emma the pen and paper. "Could you write down the ingredients I tell you?"

Emma winced. "I don't have very good handwriting."

"Pish. My handwriting would make a nun weep. I'm sure yours is better." Mr. Crackle went to the large cabinet and swung open the doors. He lifted his index finger to the top left and gently moved it across the rows of ingredients. As he contemplated the hundreds of clear, neatly shelved bottles, Emma and Albie stood beside him and looked at some of the typed labels:

MOONBEAM EXTRACT

ESSENCE OF BUBBLE FLOWER

WATERFALL CREAM

BABBLEBERRY JUICE

FIREROCK POWDER—CAUTION: FLABBABLE

"What in flames is *flabbable*?" asked Albie.

"*Flammable*. The *m* on my typewriter wasn't working the day I labeled my firerock powder, so I had to improvise." Mr. Crackle paused over a nearly empty bottle. "We need biddle hegs."

As Mr. Crackle checked the recipe against his stock of ingredients, he called out the ones they needed to buy. Emma wrote down "biddle hegs, burberry beans, a curled-up squid, gobs of trops, guzzle spleens, skibbly hoppy mead, sogs, the spizzle of a shick shack shree, a tickler's thread, whingbuzzit legs, and a wibbly cobby-seed."

She hoped she had spelled their names right.

⚹ 20 ⚹

Still Getting Ready

"That should do it, except for the spiky hat, which neither the spice shop nor I have," said Mr. Crackle as he glanced at the recipe a final time. "We'll have to make it ourselves. Harrumph. I'll probably poke myself grumpy."

Emma jumped. "I don't think so—my parents gave me a prickled hat as a going-away present. It has cactus spines and everything."

Albie looked aghast. "Your parents gave you that cactus-prickled hat for a *going-away present*?!"

Emma shrugged. "Mom and Dad said prickles are all the rage in Paris."

Mr. Crackle said slowly and carefully, "Emma, your parents are nitwits."

Emma smiled. "Thanks, Mr. Crackle."

"Now then. Let's get this recipe cracking. Here's the plan. You and Albie nip off to your uncle's house and grab your prickled hat. While you're there, you might as well bring that wooden backpack box you use for your uncle's desserts. Some of the ingredients we need must not be squished or they'll explode. In the meantime, I'll see what I can do to translate this recipe into understandable English. And do please be speedy. I believe I can no longer taste the hint of peanut butter that was sticking on my tongue not a minute ago."

"We'll be back in half an hour," Emma declared.

"Tops," promised Albie.

They grabbed their coats and hurried out the door as Mr. Crackle went upstairs to consult *The Encyclopedia of Eccentric Baking Terms.*

✦ 21 ✦

The Prickled Hat

Emma and Albie raced down the main street, up the dirt driveway, and into Uncle Simon's house. As they entered, they heard Uncle Simon and Maximus jabbering away in the living room. Albie tiptoed to the kitchen pantry, while Emma crept to her room. She crouched next to her bed and found the loathsome birthday hat in the darkest, dustiest corner. Gingerly she picked it up and immediately pricked her fingers. Gritting her teeth, she placed the hat into an empty cardboard box. When she exited her room, she found Albie, who had hauled the dessert box to the porch. "Let's go!" he whispered.

Emma got ready to hitch the box over her shoulders, but suddenly she stopped.

She was staring at a pair of hunting boots and pointy white shoes on the front porch.

Her fingers smarted. Her mind whirled.

She opened the shoe box full of prickled hat. She

carefully broke off a couple of spines and dropped them into Uncle Simon's boots and Maximus Beedy's shoes.

Albie gave a quiet giggle. "That'll get them hopping." He peered into the shoes. "Hang on—those prickles won't do any pricking lying flat. Let me spike them up a bit."

Emma grinned. "I'll keep an eye out," she whispered.

"Will do," Albie whispered back.

Emma crept over to the living room window and took a quick peek inside. She saw Uncle Simon lounging on the couch in front of the television, stuffing himself with mashed liver and a box of chocolates. His bulging eyes were riveted to a show on meat marinades. Maximus Beedy perched stick-straight on a chair next to Uncle Simon. With one hand he dipped a small cloth into a jar of polish for his cane. As Maximus turned the cane, it reflected the sun onto the television screen.

Uncle Simon snapped, "Beedy, if you don't stop moving that blasted cane and interrupting my program, I will move it somewhere where it won't be so shiny. Like the *garbage disposal*."

"Obviously you have no sense of style, Simon," Maximus hissed. "This cane is made out of the finest rare metals brought up from the bowels of the earth. I polish it with a combination of crocodile wax and the tears of small orphans. Most people would sell their grandmothers for a cane this lustrous."

Uncle Simon finished his liver and chocolate with a

gulp. "Lustrous or not, it's bugging the nose hairs out of me."

"Which wouldn't be a bad thing," Maximus sneered.

Uncle Simon stood up. "Maximus, you are becoming a most unwanted houseguest. I do hope your little scheme doesn't take much time," he snarled, "because if it does, the only thing shiny you'll have is a shiner of a dented eye." He shuffled toward the door. "I'm going to check my rabbit traps. When I get back, you had better be done polishing your cane."

Emma glanced back at Albie. He was still crouched next to the shoes, delicately arranging the prickles in them. "Uncle Simon's coming!" Emma whispered urgently.

"Give me one more minute!" Albie whispered back. "I'm almost done!"

Emma burst into the house and ran down the hallway. She flung open the living room door just as Uncle Simon was about to open it. He burped in surprise as she bustled in and slammed the door shut.

"Made the elixir yet, brat?" Uncle Simon barked. A small piece of chocolaty meat flew from his mouth and landed on Emma's shoe.

Emma kicked it off with a jerk. "Not yet. I needed to get the dessert box for Mr. Crackle."

"Going to make a magical elixir with an oversized box? You must be dimmer than I thought." Uncle Simon guffawed.

Behind them, Maximus gave a cry of rage. The

spit-and-chocolate-covered meat Emma had flicked had landed on the tip-top of his cane. "Simon! Something foul has just landed on my cane and ruined my afternoon's worth of polishing! Ugh! It smells like your lunch!"

Uncle Simon arched an eyebrow. He walked over to Maximus, plucked the chewed-up bit, and popped it into his mouth. "Waste not, want not!" he purred.

Maximus's eyes burned. He lifted his cane and twisted the top gently into Uncle Simon's enormous gut. "One day, Simon," he said slowly, "I may cure you of your love of food."

"Sticky buns and rat rubbish!" snorted Uncle Simon. "Impossible!"

Maximus twisted a little more. "Once we've made our fortune, I suggest you watch what you eat. You never know when a little poison might slip into your meat."

Emma decided it was a good time to make her exit. "Bye, Uncle Simon! See you tomorrow!" She left Uncle Simon and Maximus glaring at each other and darted out of the room. Albie was standing on the front porch with the shoe box. He winked. "All set!"

Emma clasped her hands and shook them high in the air. Then she grabbed the dessert box and slung it onto her back. The two of them hurried back to Mr. Crackle's, whistling cheerfully all the way.

✦ 22 ✦

Down the Flour Barrel

When Emma and Albie returned to the cake shop, they found Mr. Crackle upstairs, busily clicking away at his rickety typewriter. He tapped a final letter, pulled the paper from the roller, and pocketed it. "All set! Let's go downstairs and find ourselves a spice shop!"

Mr. Crackle led the way down to the enormous flour barrel. He lifted off the lid and beckoned. "Take a look," he said.

Emma and Albie peered down. Tiny flickering lamps glowed against a sturdy metal ladder that led down a deep tunnel. The tunnel stretched farther than they could see.

Emma heard a soft click. She turned to see Mr. Crackle with his finger on a little switch attached to the kitchen wall. A whoosh of air came sliding up the barrel.

Mr. Crackle slung the dessert box onto his back. He adjusted the straps, then gave a quick wiggle so the box settled comfortably on his shoulders.

"Okay, you two," he said. "Down we go! Don't worry

about falling—the tunnel has a rising jet of air that will buoy you up if you accidentally slip. I'll go first. After one minute, Emma, you can hop in. Albie, wait a minute more, then follow."

He hitched one leg, then the other, into the barrel.

Emma and Albie heard the *clink, clink* of his feet on the metal bars. After the second hand on the kitchen clock wheeled around, Emma climbed into the barrel.

Down she went. She could feel the upwind cushioning her feet with every step, but she didn't quite trust it to hold her.

The air grew cool, then cold, but the small, cheery lamps lit the way. Emma put her hand out to touch the tunnel wall, which felt like smooth rock. There was nothing to hold on to but the ladder.

A voice floated up from below. "You're doing wonderfully, Emma! Just a couple hundred steps more to go!"

Down.

Down.

Down she went.

The farther down Emma went, the more the plume of air tugged at her. She had to tighten her grip on the ladder's rungs to keep from being pulled upward.

Just when her hands started to go numb from clutching the cold metal, her right foot met solid dirt. Shakily, she stepped off the ladder with her other foot.

She glanced behind her.

At her feet, a giant circular grate covered an enormous

fan silently spinning at a terrific speed. Emma realized that the fan was what created the updraft in the tunnel.

"Well done!" Mr. Crackle grinned at her, a few feet from the outer ridge of the grate. "Now edge sideways until you're out of the way of the air current."

Emma noticed that the metal rungs of the ladder had shifted sideways, only a few feet above the dirt floor. Carefully gripping the rungs, Emma edged away from the grate, until she was standing next to Mr. Crackle.

"Whew! That was a bit tricky!" Albie popped up next to the two of them and wiped his brow.

Mr. Crackle tugged at a switch on the tunnel wall. With a jerk, the enormous fan came to a halt and the blast of air died down.

Emma let go of the breath she had been holding. She took a look around her.

Hundreds of tiny lamps lit up a circular underground tunnel. On the tunnel's outer edge, identical ladders descended to the floor, stretching fifty feet apart and disappearing into the curve of the tunnel.

Massive oaken doors with wrought-iron handles ringed the tunnel's inner edge. Perched above each handle was a small pipe that led to a glass chamber filled with loops of metal wire that curled out in all directions. Mr. Crackle led Emma and Albie to a door a few feet from where they had descended. He stopped and fiddled in his pocket, frowning as he concentrated.

Albie gaped at the door. "That's fancy!" He whistled.

"These aren't the kinds of doors I've ever knocked on before! What's that funny glass box full of metal stuff for?"

"It's a breath-recognition system—aha, here it is!" said Mr. Crackle. He withdrew a green velvet bag from his pocket and tipped it over. A silver key fell into his palm. "Each Supreme-Extreme Master gets a ladder and a specialized door to enter the spice shop."

"Why doesn't the spice shop have just one door?" Emma asked.

"Security—each door is locked and can only be opened by a Supreme-Extreme Master. To open my door, I turn the lock with this key, then breathe into the pipe. Things click, and the door opens. It's a piece of engineering I don't understand, but it works beautifully. By the way, make sure you don't touch the door. The engineers told me strange things will happen to anyone other than me who does."

"What happens?" Emma asked.

"I don't have a smack of a clue, but I don't want you to be the one who finds out."

Emma and Albie stood back as Mr. Crackle slipped the key into the lock and turned it twice. He blew into the glass tube, misting the inside. There was a whirring of bolts and locks, and he pulled the door open.

They stepped through.

23

The Spice Shop

Emma's nose quivered as she inhaled sharp, strange, witchy aromas. She looked around and drew a small, quiet breath.

She was surrounded by thousands and thousands of spices. Packed in glass jars on shelves that reached far up beyond her sight, they filled the shop with dusty browns, brilliant oranges, deep blues, cool greens, rich reds, and brilliant golds. Emma had never seen more colors in her life. She saw powders and liquids and jellies and shriveled dried twisted things with sockets that might have once held eyeballs. The ingredients jostled and jumbled her senses, until she couldn't tell if she was breathing in color or tasting smells.

Emma felt she had just begun to touch the tip of a vast and ancient world. A curl of excitement grew in her stomach as she ran her fingers over the jars, reading and looking and sniffing.

"What do you think?" whispered Mr. Crackle.

"It's marvelous," Emma whispered back.

"'Magical," whispered Albie.

"What's all this whispering about?" whispered a fourth voice.

With a start, Emma, Albie, and Mr. Crackle jolted around. The dessert box, still strapped to Mr. Crackle's back, swung into a jar filled with pale yellow grains. The jar plunged to the ground.

Two inches from the floor, a hand shot underneath the jar and brought it firmly upward, back to the shelf.

"Gregor Crackle, mind that thing on your back," scolded a tiny woman with tortoiseshell glasses and dark red hair. She slid the jar back into place, then turned to her visitors. "You are an exceptionally careful man, and I would expect no less of you while in my shop. I do apologize for startling you. Now, please introduce me to your friends and let me know how I can help."

"Hello, Mabel. You're just as to the point as I remember." Mr. Crackle gingerly unstrapped the dessert box and set it on the floor. "Mabel, meet Emma and Albie. Albie's my official cutter control person—he keeps the snooty people in line. Emma's a lovely young lady whose unlovely uncle is forcing me to make the Elixir of Delight. Emma and Albie, meet Mabel, a dear friend who won the Supreme-Extreme Master of the Kitchen Contest a year before I did. She remembers recipes frighteningly well."

Mabel looked sternly at Mr. Crackle. "Gregor, stop

trying to flatter me. I was born with a photographic memory, that's all." Her eyebrows arched. "How the devil did you get your fingers on the Elixir of Delight recipe? If I remember my cooking history lessons correctly, it was buried in the catacombs under Tuptiddy City in AD 18 and no one has seen it since."

"I received the recipe from a very unpleasant man who poisoned me and won't give me the antidote until I make him the elixir."

"You seem remarkably unflustered about being poisoned, Gregor." Mabel lifted her eyebrows. "What exactly were you poisoned with?"

"Joobajooba extract."

"Joobajooba extract?" Mabel frowned. "Is it compounded with anything?"

"Powdered wolf fangs and nightshade."

"Hmm. How ironic."

"How so?" asked Mr. Crackle.

"The unpleasant man who poisoned you does not have the antidote."

"What?!"

"The antidote requires the Elixir of Delight."

"What?!"

"By itself, joobajooba extract is combatable by a simple mixture of sugar and pickled cabbage juice, but if you add wolf fangs and nightshade, you also need ten drops of the Elixir of Delight to properly get rid of the poison."

"WHAT?!"

Mabel sighed. "Gregor, you sound like a squawking duck."

"Sorry, but where— How do you know this?"

"I read books. The antidote is in the 1567 edition of *Lugo Looby's Obscure Poisons and Their Antidotes.* I wouldn't worry, though. You are a smart and capable baker and should have no trouble making the elixir. Now, let's see your shopping list."

Mr. Crackle's hands shook as he gave Mabel the list. She lifted up her glasses and studied it.

Emma went up to Mr. Crackle. He looked down at her.

Emma took his hands and gave them a squeeze. She said softly, "Don't worry, Mr. Crackle. You're the best baker in the world. If anyone can make this elixir, it's you."

Albie chimed in, "Mr. Crackle, you'll be drinking that elixir and getting back your senses faster than a bee on honey. After all, you're a Supreme-Extreme Master!"

Mr. Crackle smiled. "Thank you," he said. He returned Emma's squeeze and straightened his long back. "I do believe I've got the best assistants any winner of the Supreme-Extreme Master of the Kitchen Contest could choose."

Emma smiled. Suddenly something in her head jiggled. "Mr. Crackle?"

"Yes, Emma?"

"Do you know someone named Maddie Tinkleberry?"

Mr. Crackle's eyes lit up. "Last year's Supreme-Extreme winner? Of course I do! Maddie is a very talented young woman. She and I once worked on a chocolate soufflé for the Queen of Bavaria's eightieth birthday. At the last moment, she decided to add tickleberry rose extract to the batter. The soufflé came out quite perfect."

"Do you know where she is?"

Mr. Crackle wrinkled his eyebrows. "The last time I saw her, she was about to leave for France to search for a rare ingredient—a mysterious kind of berry, I believe. She was in a great hurry."

Emma swallowed hard. "Mr. Beedy said she made the Elixir of Delight for him and then she disappeared. For months he tried to hunt her down to make sure she wouldn't tell about the elixir, but he never found her."

Mabel clucked. "I should have known that Maddie would get herself into a cooking adventure."

Mr. Crackle frowned. "What do you mean?"

"Maddie Tinkleberry does not like cheaters when it comes to food." Mabel drew a finger down Mr. Crackle's list as she scanned the ingredients. "When she created the Elixir of Delight, she must have realized that any mediocre cook with a dose of it would be unstoppable." Her finger slowly made its way toward the bottom of the list. "My bet is that she's looking for starberries in France. They have the most curious ability to reveal the true talent of a cook. Starberries turn anything that is not superb into a bland mush, but for a truly delicious creation, they enhance the flavors to an astonishing degree."

She pushed her glasses firmly up her nose. "I've finished

reading your list. It will only take me a few moments to gather these ingredients. In the meantime, why don't you sit down a spell and take a breather—it'll do you good before you attempt the recipe." She turned to Emma and Albie. "You two should feel free to take a look around. But make sure you don't taste anything. Some ingredients here are delightful in pies but deadly on their own."

✦ 24 ✦

Spice Exploration

Mabel pushed a comfy chair next to the spice shop's front counter and gave Mr. Crackle an aspirin. "Sit," she commanded.

Mr. Crackle sat.

As Mabel bustled off to find the elixir ingredients, she called to Emma and Albie, "Feel free to look around, but remember—if you try anything, you will most likely regret it."

Emma and Albie wandered into an aisle. There was so much to look at. Emma took a jar of green crystals off the shelf. She saw a label on the cover: MOON SUGAR. "So this is what Mr. Crackle puts in his truffles!" she exclaimed.

"Ooooh, look at this one!" Albie said, tapping a bottle filled with golden syrup. "It's called African billooflower honey. I bet it'd be tasty on crackers!"

Emma reached for a jar labeled KOOLAKOOLA TREE BARK. She sat down and twisted off the lid, then reached in to feel

the thick, dark chunks of bark. The rough, rich-smelling squares crumbled in her hand.

She wanted badly to take a tiny taste, but she remembered how dangerous ingredients could be. With a sigh, she screwed the lid back on the jar.

As she stood up, she heard a quick, strange sound.

Thump.

Silence.

Thump.

Silence.

Albie cocked his ear. "Something's moving about."

THUMP THUMP THUMP THUMP THUMP.

Emma and Albie jumped. They followed the thumps to the middle of the aisle. All of a sudden, the shelves ended, leaving a deep, wide space.

Inside the space was an enormous glass jar.

Inside the jar, giant, pink, warty blobs dashed against the glass at terrific speeds. Emma watched as they hit the jar and flattened like pancakes before pulling themselves into blobs again and zinging to the other side.

"Aha! There you are." Mabel strode down the aisle. "I've got all your ingredients but the biddle hegs—oh, you've found them!" She popped open the enormous jar and whistled a strange, high note three times.

Three of the pink blobs zoomed out of the jar and landed with a *thump thump thump* in her hand. Mabel neatly tipped them into a box and sealed it. "And that should do it!" She checked a tiny silver watch that dangled from her slim wrist. "Now, I know Gregor will be eager to get to work on the elixir, but I think we have a few moments for you two to see the best part of this place." She beckoned to Emma and Albie. "Come this way."

They followed her to a corner of the shop, where a thick black curtain hung over a doorway.

"Step through, please," said Mabel.

Through they went.

They were in a pitch-black room. The sights and sounds and smells of the spice shop entirely disappeared. "Close your eyes for ten seconds to let them adjust, then open them," Mabel said.

Emma shut her eyes, counted, and then slowly opened them. And for the second time that day, she took a small, quiet breath.

She was surrounded by glowing, swirling flecks of colored light. They pooled and eddied softly inside glass bottles, bumping one another with the gentleness of floating bubbles. They looked weightless and very, very fragile.

"They're lovely," Albie sighed.

"What are they?" whispered Emma.

"Dust from the aurora borealis. They can only be gathered at midnight at the winter solstice."

"What do they do?"

"They make anything taste as light as air."

Emma watched the gleaming speckles shimmer and

dance. She wondered whether she would see anything more beautiful in her life.

"Makes you glad to be alive," Mabel said softly.

They stood silently, until they heard Mabel say gently, "Time to go."

Tugging their eyes away, Emma and Albie headed back to the lights and smells of the spice shop.

✳ 25 ✳

Mr. Crackle's Past Mistakes

When they returned to the spice-shop counter, Emma, Albie, and Mabel found Mr. Crackle looking slightly better. As Mabel packaged their ingredients into neatly labeled jars and plastic packets, Mr. Crackle brought over the dessert box. Once the jars and packets had been labeled, he slid them inside.

"Make sure you separate the biddle hegs from the wibbly cobbyseed," cautioned Mabel.

"What will happen if we don't?" asked Emma.

"If they touch each other, they form a vapor that turns your head into a pumpkin. It's painful."

"Oh," said Emma.

"Don't worry, in all the years I've known him, Gregor has made only two cooking mistakes," said Mabel.

Mr. Crackle, who had just finished putting the last ingredient in the box, suddenly looked uncomfortable. "Now, Mabel, there's no need to talk about the past."

Mabel's lips twitched, just slightly. "Suit yourself."

"What did you do, Mr. Crackle?" Albie asked. "Did you ever give anyone a case of the runs?"

Mr. Crackle sighed. "It was a little more dramatic. I once overestimated the amount of aurora borealis dust I was supposed to put in a chocolate soufflé."

Albie's eyes widened. "Is that the same dust we just saw?"

Mabel nodded. "It is a beautiful but dangerously potent ingredient."

"What happens when you eat too much?" Emma asked.

Mr. Crackle dropped his head. "The fellow who ate the soufflé shrank to the size of a gingerbread man and floated out of the shop. I had to chase him down with a butterfly net and feed him rock candy to put him right."

"And what was your second mistake?" Mabel's lips twitched into a full-on smile.

Mr. Crackle looked pained. "Last year I turned all the Supreme-Extreme Masters into fudge Popsicles. I miscalculated how much babbleberry juice to put in the punch for an annual cooking convention."

"And how long did it take you to turn those Popsicles back into people?" asked Mabel. Her voice was very, very sweet.

"Three days." Mr. Crackle paused. "I had to share some very secret recipes to calm a few tempers."

Mabel laughed. "Every person, no matter how talented, makes mistakes. And there's nothing wrong with that. Good luck, Gregor. Remember: You can get rid of the poison inside you with a cup of sugar, a cup of pickled cabbage, and ten drops of the Elixir of Delight. I know you hate pickled cabbage, but under the circumstances, I would make an exception."

Mr. Crackle grimaced. He hitched up the dessert box, and he, Albie, and Emma waved goodbye to Mabel as they swung open the spice-shop door and climbed back up the tunnel to their own world.

✦ 26 ✦

A Little Translating

They emerged from the flour barrel to find the last rays of sunset disappearing from the kitchen windows.

Albie glanced at the clock. "Yipes! I need to get home—my parents will be worried."

Mr. Crackle rested the ingredient box on the counter. "Albie, do you think your parents would mind if you spent the night here? We'll need to start making the elixir early tomorrow if we're going to have it ready by noon."

"Well, my dad might ask for some free cookies. . . ."

"Done."

"Great! I'll give them a call."

While Albie phoned his parents, Mr. Crackle and Emma went to the attic and dug up a sleeping bag and an inflatable mattress for him. After eating a quick dinner, with crème brûlée for dessert, they settled in for the night. Mr. Crackle tucked Emma and Albie in and read them a story from a slim book called *Top Ten Cooking Disasters*. Halfway through a story about a wayward blueberry coffee cake, he stopped with a jolt. "Well, what an odd sensation. I can't feel this book anymore. There goes my sense of touch."

The two children stared.

"Albie and Emma!" Mr. Crackle said sharply. "If your eyes get any bigger, they're going to pop out of your head." He flipped a page of the book. "Don't worry, you two—if I can still turn pages, I can still make recipes. If I go blind, that'll be tricky, but since the next sense to go is my hearing, you two won't have anything to worry about. I've always been a little deaf anyway."

And he went back to reading.

That night, Emma dreamed of floating colored speckles and being chased by a gigantic coffee cake.

Early the next morning, Emma and Albie woke to the smells of tea and toast.

"Good morning!" Mr. Crackle appeared with a breakfast tray and placed it on the table for them. After Emma and Albie wolfed down their meal, he gave them the translated recipe he had typed out the day before. "Take a look at this, then come downstairs. I'm going to sort the ingredients in the kitchen," he said, and headed downstairs.

Emma and Albie read the translated page:

Blend together two burberry beans, a curled-up squid, and five guzzle spleens. Liquefy ten whingbuzzit legs, a sack of sogs, and three biddle hegs. Lightly fry the mizzle of a jug-jug tree. Burn to a crisp the spizzle of a shick shack shree. Chop, dice, mince, then puree ten tooby tibs of timtam tea. Crush a wibbly cobbyseed; heat a skibbly hoppy mead to boiling; add a splash of juice and a dozen fribs. Mix everything together.

Go outside and check the weather. If it's raining, catch six drops and add to six gobs of trops. If it's sunny, catch a ray and shine it in three dozen drops of blay. Add to the burberry mixture, stir twelve times clockwise, twelve times counterclockwise, turn upside down twice, and shake. Heat the mixture to boiling, then add the gloamy foamy ball of a chixed-up, fixed-up spider shawl. Stir until the liquid turns brown; cool 2.6.3 degrees. Pour into a spiky hat, kick the hat three times, then sift the mixture through a red tickler's thread. Add lifflets until Emma and Albie like the taste.

Emma squinted. Mr. Crackle had written something at the bottom of the recipe in strange, scrawly letters. She had to tilt her head and shut an eye to figure out the handwriting but eventually made out the extra note:

Don't eat at noon.

✳ 27 ✳

Burberry Beans and Wibbly Cobbyseed

Finished reading, Emma and Albie went down to the kitchen and found that Mr. Crackle had spread the jars and packets of ingredients out on the counter. Emma hadn't had time to see them properly in the spice shop, but now she gazed in wonder as the morning light reflected their bizarre colors and shapes. Burberry beans gleamed bright purple next to the pink, blobby biddle hegs. The spizzle of a shick shack shree looked like a twisty silver-flecked ribbon, wiggling in its packet. Whingbuzzit legs were lumpish and gray, and the wibbly cobbyseed had thousands of tiny grooves etched into its turquoise shell.

When Emma finally lifted her eyes from the counter, she found Mr. Crackle rummaging through a cupboard above the oven. With an "Aha!" he pulled down a massive blender with wickedly sharp blades. "Emma, do you know how to operate one of these?" he asked.

Emma nodded. "Yup. Every Tuesday, Uncle Simon makes me mix up five butter and lard milkshakes for his afternoon snack."

Albie gagged. "Butter and lard milkshakes?"

Emma sighed. "They're awfully thick."

Mr. Crackle said, "Your uncle is awfully thick. Well, why don't you and Albie plug in the blender and take care of the beans, squid, spleens, legs, sogs, and hegs, while I deal with the tree, shick shack shree spizzle, and tea."

While Emma and Albie blended and liquefied, Mr. Crackle fried and chopped, sliced and diced, minced and pureed. Colors whirled and crackled into one another as the three worked. A dark, sour, stinging odor filled the air, and violent blue smoke poured out of the frying pan into the kitchen. The spizzle of the shick shack shree hissed and spat in a gigantic pan, hopping and dancing like popcorn over a roasting fire.

"How're you doing?" shouted Mr. Crackle.

"Fine," Emma yelled.

"What?"

"Fine!"

"WHAT?"

"FINE!"

"OH DEAR, I'VE GONE DEAF! JUST TAP ME ON THE SHOULDER WHEN YOU'RE DONE!"

Albie and Emma looked at each other.

Time was running out.

They waited impatiently until the biddle hegs sloshed

evenly with the whingbuzzit legs and sogs, then jammed off the blender. Albie dashed the blenderful of ingredients over to Mr. Crackle and nearly bashed into the stove in his haste. Emma put out a hand to steady him, then used her other hand to poke Mr. Crackle on the shoulder.

Mr. Crackle turned and grinned. "Excellent! Look for a mortar and pestle in the third cupboard to the left of the fridge. Once you find it, grind the wibbly cobbyseed to smithereens—the powder should be lemon yellow when you're done."

Albie collected the wibbly cobbyseed while Emma found the mortar and pestle. Albie dropped the cobbyseed into the stone bowl, and Emma raised the pestle high. With a *WHAP!* she brought the pestle down and broke the turquoise shell. Hundreds of tiny dark pink stones poured out. As she crushed them, the stones broke into smaller, sharp black shards, then were pulverized into a soft yellow powder. A rich, nutty scent drifted into the air, and the powder crackled like chestnuts snapping in a hot pan.

When the last of the black shards had crumbled into yellow, Emma tapped the pestle against the mortar to free the last bits of powder. She heaved the bowl up to the counter, then joined Mr. Crackle at the stove.

Huge blue flames danced underneath a copper skillet bubbling with a clear gooey liquid. Mr. Crackle had just put down a bottle labeled JUICE and had dipped his hand into a basket full of clicking balls that looked like marbles. "Fribs," he explained as he tossed twelve into the skillet.

The fribs dissolved into the liquid, which started to swirl, slowly at first, then faster and faster, until it whirled and rose up to become a two-foot tornado spinning in the exact center of the skillet.

"Quick! Hand me the cobbyseed!"

Albie gave the stone bowl to Mr. Crackle, who tipped the powder into the funnel of the tornado. There was a *BANG!* The liquid shot up three feet more, then fell back down into the skillet and began to simmer softly.

Mr. Crackle picked up a wooden spoon in one hand and a frying pan full of ingredients in the other. He tilted the pan's gloppy, purply contents into the skillet and stirred. The mixture turned slime green and kept simmering.

As he stirred, Mr. Crackle shouted to Emma and Albie, "The next ingredient we need depends on the weather. Take a peek out the window and see if it's sunny or rainy. If there's sun, we'll need to use a raycatcher. If it's rainy, you'll need to catch six drops."

Albie gave Emma a fearful look. "What if it's cloudy but not raining?"

Emma shuddered. "Let's not worry about that until we've looked outside."

They went to the window and opened the shutters.

Warm morning sunlight slanted onto their faces. They returned to Mr. Crackle.

"Sunny," Emma mouthed to Mr. Crackle.

He nodded. "Sunlight and blay it is! The raycatcher is in the cupboard next to the spice cabinet. It looks like a

wire whisk with a glass ball poking out from the top. Go outside and aim the glass toward the sun. Wait until it turns orange, then bring it inside."

Albie went to the cupboard and yanked out the ray-catcher. He and Emma ran outside.

"How much time do you think Mr. Crackle has left before he goes blind?" Albie asked as he aimed the ray-catcher at the sun.

Emma stared ferociously at the raycatcher, willing the glass ball to change color. "I don't know, but I don't want to find out. Hurry, sun, *hurry*!"

After a minute, the raycatcher ball started to glint and glimmer. Yellow swirls clouded the glass. The swirls grew thicker and thicker, then abruptly burst into an orange glow.

With a whoop, Albie and Emma rushed back into the kitchen, the raycatcher blazing orange. Mr. Crackle had taken the skillet off the stove, and it lay cooling on the counter. The baker stood hunched over a saucer next to the skillet with an eyedropper full of amber fluid. A bottle marked BLAY sat next to his elbow. Carefully he squeezed thirty-six drops into the saucer. He took the raycatcher and touched the glass to the liquid. With a *whoosh,* a beam of light shot out of the glass. It shone straight at the ceiling for a moment, then bent and twisted down in a ribbon to curl around the liquid blay. The blay turned solid and began to glow.

Mr. Crackle picked up the glowing blay and plopped it

into the skillet. He took his spoon and gave it twelve stirs clockwise and twelve stirs counterclockwise. The concoction had turned into a weird wobbly lime Jell-O with blue sparks dancing off the surface.

"Emma, hand me a cutting board!"

Emma took a board off a shelf by the oven and gave it to Mr. Crackle. He placed the board on top of the skillet, flipped the skillet, then flipped the board so the ingredients landed back in the skillet. He slid the contents into a wide-mouthed bottle, capped the bottle, and handed it to Albie. "Give this a good shake until you see bubbles."

Albie shook the mixture until it became liquid and turned a frothy green, then gave it to Mr. Crackle. He uncapped the bottle and poured the contents into the pot on the stove, then turned on the heat. When the mixture was bubbling and boiling, he added a webby mass of a balled-up sticky spider shawl and started to stir. Once the liquid turned brown, he switched off the heat and stuck a thermometer into the pot.

"Emma, it's time to make use of that prickled hat your parents gave you!" Mr. Crackle shouted. "We'll need to pour this brew into it. I'm afraid the hat will be ruined."

"Thank goodness," said Emma. She flew upstairs to retrieve the hat, then brought it to the kitchen and placed it on the floor. Mr. Crackle gave the thermometer a final swirl in the potion, studied it, then swooped the pot off the stove and dumped its contents into the hat. He gave the hat three good kicks. The liquid popped and fizzled, and the cactus prickles on the outside of the hat turned silver.

He brought the hat up to the counter, where a tickler's thread lay like a mesh over a small bowl. He tipped the hat over. Out spilled a cup of bright green mush. Mr. Crackle took a paddle and gently pressed the mush against the tickler's thread. A copper-tinted liquid dripped down and collected at the bottom of the bowl.

"It is a rare sight, to see so many colors in one day," Mr. Crackle said softly. "Sometimes I feel like an alchemist of years gone by, mixing the elements of the world."

✳28✳

Lifflets

When the last of the liquid had strained through, Mr. Crackle slid the thread off the top of the bowl. "Time for the final ingredient! Have I ever told you two about lifflets?"

Emma and Albie shook their heads.

"Lifflets are tiny whorls of air that dance over Mipplymoo's Bayou. Devilishly difficult to catch. It was years before I figured out how."

Mr. Crackle went to the corner of the kitchen and began to knock a knuckle up and down the wall. "To trap them, you have to wait until one is right by your mouth, then—*whoop!*—you suck in quick, then—*whoosh!*—blow out into a bottle, and if you're lucky, you've got one."

His knuckle thunked against a hollow spot. "Aha!" He tapped three times on the spot, and two doors opened out, revealing a hollow in the wall. "This is where I keep my most precious ingredients." Mr. Crackle reached in and drew out a blue bottle with an enormously long neck.

Emma and Albie could see wisps of something bumping madly around inside.

"Lifflets add excitement to any dish you cook up," said Mr. Crackle. "They whirl over your tongue like a mini-hurricane, and before long, your taste buds are dancing and so are you! I use them in lollipops for special occasions, like fiftieth wedding anniversaries. They make grandmas dance especially fast."

Mr. Crackle opened a cupboard door and pulled out a long tube looped into dozens of coils. He reached back into the cupboard and fished around until he found a cap no bigger than the eye of a darning needle. "Here's what we need to do. I'm going to cap one end of this tube, then open the lifflet bottle and stick the other end of the tube down the bottle's neck. I want you to shake the bottle gently, as if you're trying to wake up a sleeping butterfly inside you. That tiny bit of movement should dislodge only one lifflet, which will come whizzing through the tube. I'll uncap the tube to let the lifflet through. Make sure you shake the bottle as carefully as you can, or you may disturb more than one lifflet."

Mr. Crackle put the lifflet bottle and elixir bowl next to one another. Delicately he opened the bottle and wedged the tube inside. He held the other end of the tube in one hand; the other hand rested on the cap. He gave Emma a smile and a nod.

Emma held the bottle and gave it a featherlight shake.

The tube shook violently. A lifflet wriggled through,

quick as lightning. Emma held her breath. The lifflet shot through the loops and landed with a *flump!* in the elixir. Mr. Crackle flicked his wrist and capped the tube.

Emma peered into the bowl. The liquid had become a copper whirlpool. It spun so fast it whistled; then, with a soft thump, it settled and became still.

Mr. Crackle brought out an eyedropper. "Give it a taste."

Emma and Albie dipped the dropper into the liquid, then squirted a tiny drop onto their tongues. Albie made a horrific grimace. Emma winced and shook her head. "Ugh. Flat soda pop."

Mr. Crackle frowned. "Vats full of cod? That doesn't sound right. Let's see what your tongues look like."

Emma and Albie stuck out their tongues. Mr. Crackle studied them.

"Hmm. Looks perfectly pink to me. Let's add another lifflet."

One by one, Mr. Crackle and Emma dropped lifflets into the elixir. Each time Emma and Albie took a taste, the mixture got worse. After flat soda pop, they tasted musty mothballs, a wormy apple, and burned plastic. There wasn't the slightest speck of yellow on their tongues.

Then, while they were adding the fifth lifflet, the accident happened.

✴ 29 ✴

The Last Step

Emma didn't mean to jiggle the lifflet bottle as hard as she did. It's just that when you're racing to save the best baker in the world, and you have the ugly taste of flat pop, and mothballs, and bad apples, and burned plastic in your mouth, you get rather annoyed.

It's one thing to ask a child to taste different kinds of lollipops to see which one she likes best. It's another to ask her to taste a potion that keeps getting worse.

Emma had more patience than most ten-year-olds, but the burned plastic was just too much.

"Rotten lifflets," she muttered. "I'll show them."

When it came time to wiggle the bottle a fifth time, with a horrible taste in her mouth and a grim smile on her face, Emma gave the bottle a firm and violent shake.

Every single lifflet shot through the tube.

"Uh-oh," said Mr. Crackle.

He jammed the cap onto the tube.

The lifflets buried themselves against the cap, pushing

with all their might to burst free. The tube grew bloated and puffy, stretching thinner and thinner and bigger and bigger. . . .

Pop! went the cap. *Whoooosh!* went the lifflets! Into the elixir they flew, bright strands of purple and gold that twinkled and shimmered and swirled and then . . . disappeared.

The elixir turned black. Foul green smoke poured from the bowl, and a vicious odor sprang up. Coughing and sputtering, Mr. Crackle ran to a window and wrenched it open. Emma and Albie followed at his heels, and the three of them gulped in the outside air.

"I didn't mean to shake . . . well, I did mean to . . . but burned plastic . . . I'm so sorry!" sobbed Emma.

"My dear Emma, don't look so forlorn," wheezed Mr. Crackle. "Perhaps you saved us some time and gave the elixir just the right amount of lifflets with one good shake."

They waited until the smoke cleared; then gingerly they peeked back into the kitchen. With a dreadful feeling in her stomach, Emma followed Mr. Crackle to the counter where the elixir was.

Mr. Crackle peered into the bowl. He started, then furrowed his eyebrows. "Hmm. Emma, Albie, take a look at this." He lowered the bowl so they could peer into it.

The liquid had turned utterly still. It was as pure and clear as water.

"Let's test it," said Mr. Crackle softly.

He picked up the eyedropper and dipped it into the

bowl. Slowly, carefully, he pulled up a bit of the liquid. He squeezed a single drop onto Emma's tongue, then Albie's.

Emma was floating, weightless in the delight of the most exquisite flavor. The potion twinkled like stars in her mouth. She breathed a slow, magical breath.

It was perfect.

Mr. Crackle went to a drawer and pulled out two small mirrors. Solemnly he handed them to Emma and Albie.

Emma opened her mouth and looked at her reflection. In the center of her tongue, there gleamed a small, sparkling gold mark. She turned to Albie.

His tongue was out.

And glittering.

Emma, Albie, and Mr. Crackle looked at one another. Slowly, slowly, they started to grin, their smiles spreading and stretching wider and wider until they were laughing hard enough to hiccup. The tall baker picked up the two children and whirled them around and around until Emma felt as if she would burst with happiness.

"Now," said Mr. Crackle once he had put them down, "let's mix up some sugar and pickled cabbage and see if we can't stop that poison before my world poofs out completely."

A few minutes later, they were staring at a bowl of pink pickled cabbage crusted with sugar crystals. Mr. Crackle looked a little green.

"Why does medicine always look horrible?" he muttered as he dropped ten drops of the elixir into the bowl.

The elixir melted the sugary cabbage into a blob of red goo.

"Here goes." Mr. Crackle grimaced as he held his nose and tilted the contents of the bowl into his mouth. He swallowed.

"It worked! I've never tasted anything so foul!" he announced cheerfully. "My sense of taste is back, and so is everything else. Goodness, pickled cabbage smells atrocious!"

✦ 30 ✦

Creeker's Curse

"Time for a celebratory early lunch," Mr. Crackle declared. "I'll whip up a batch of pea soup!"

Albie and Emma exchanged glances. "Pea soup?" Albie said.

"I know it doesn't sound very exciting, but there's a reason why I was nicknamed Souper Duper in cooking school."

Half an hour later, they sat down to steaming bowls of soup and hunks of fresh bread. Mr. Crackle inhaled and smiled. "It does feel lovely to have my senses back."

As they dipped their bread into the scrumptious green soup, Emma asked hesitantly, "Mr. Crackle?"

"Yes, Emma?"

"Well, since you don't have to worry about the poison anymore, can't we just tell my uncle and Mr. Beedy that we failed to make the elixir and have done with it?"

Mr. Crackle paused thoughtfully over his soup. "Yes, we could, but I don't think that would be the end of it.

My guess is that your uncle and Maximus will do something terrible to us, whether or not we've been successful at making the elixir. We know too much of their vile plan. I don't think they'll let us go scot-free."

Albie shuddered. "Then what are we going to do?"

Mr. Crackle smiled. He dipped his hand into his pocket and withdrew the elixir recipe. He passed it to Emma and Albie. "Take a look at the last verse," he said.

Emma read the last lines of the recipe:

But, oh, beware the witchy hour
When potent powers turn sickle sour
Good shall turn from bad to worse
For those that taste at Creeker's curse.

"Where's Creeker's curse?" Emma asked.

Mr. Crackle paused. "A more accurate question would be, *What* is Creeker's curse? About five hundred years ago, there lived an extraordinary cook named Marta Creeker. Her dishes were like little mouthfuls of heaven, and people traveled thousands of miles to taste her cooking. There was one peculiar thing about her, though—she would never cook an afternoon meal."

Mr. Crackle broke off another chunk of bread and swirled it into his soup. "One day, a rich king arrived and asked Marta to be his royal chef. She said yes, on one condition—she would be responsible for his breakfast and dinner, but someone else had to cook his lunch. The king agreed. All went well for a time, but one morning the king woke up and wanted a noon feast. Unfortunately, the evening before, the royal lunch chef had become violently sick with the flu. With no other cooks around but Marta, the king demanded that she prepare the feast. When Marta reminded the king of their bargain, he flew into a fit. He threatened to throw her in a vat of bubbling oatmeal if she refused."

Albie wrinkled his nose. "Sounds like a bad case of the spoils! What happened next?"

"Marta made the feast. At noon the king sat down on his royal throne to eat. He took one bite . . . and turned into a lamb chop. It seems Marta suffered from a rare and inexplicable disease—if someone ate her food at noon, he would instantly turn into whatever he was eating." Mr. Crackle lifted his soup-sodden bread and neatly dropped it into his mouth. "Since then, any dish that shouldn't be eaten at noon has been referred to as 'Creeker's curse.'"

Emma remembered Mr. Crackle's final words to Maximus Beedy and Uncle Simon. *Come ten minutes before noon and I'll have your potion.* "Is the elixir going to turn Uncle Simon and Mr. Beedy into lamb chops?"

"The curse is a little different with every recipe. We'll just have to wait and see what happens."

They cleaned up after their lunch, then settled in to wait.

✦ 31 ✦

An Unpleasant Arrival

It was fifteen minutes before noon. Inside the cake-shop kitchen, Emma sat on the dessert box and stared at the door. Albie chewed his fingernails and paced back and forth. Mr. Crackle sat on the counter with a mug of tea.

"Do you think they're going to be on time?" Albie asked.

"They've got to be." Emma hopped down from the box and began to pace with Albie. "I wish this whole potion-drinking-at-noon didn't have to be so on-the-dot."

Mr. Crackle sipped and swallowed. "There is a certain magic in precise timing. One of my favorite parts of baking is taking a pastry out of the oven at the exact moment it is perfectly cooked."

"But if Uncle Simon and Mr. Greedy Beedy aren't exactly on time, we're the ones who'll be cooked!" Emma cried.

"Have some tea," Mr. Crackle offered. "I have a chamomile honey flavor in the cupboard that is wonderfully relaxing. And by the time you pour yourself a cup and drink it, your uncle and Mr. Beedy will be here. They know they can't be late."

Tap tap. Tap tap. Tap tap.

A cane tapped at the door.

Emma and Albie froze. Mr. Crackle smiled. "It's time." He put down his mug. "Emma, please get the door—after all, I am supposed to be deprived of most of my senses, including the ability to notice a cane tap."

Emma opened the door.

Maximus Beedy and Uncle Simon hobbled in. Maximus leaned grimly on his cane. Uncle Simon sat in a chair with a thud. "BLASTED PORCUPINE GOT ONTO THE PORCH AND SHED ALL OVER THE SHOES!" he bellowed. "I'M GOING TO HAVE THE HEAD OF EVERY PRICKLY BEAST ON MY TROPHY SHELF, IF IT'S THE LAST THING I DO!"

Emma choked back a chuckle. Behind her, Albie made a funny sound.

Maximus Beedy glared at the two children suspiciously. "You wouldn't happen to know the name of the porcupine that paid our shoes a visit, would you?"

"Well, gentlemen," Mr. Crackle said hastily, "no use chitchatting when I can't hear a word you're saying. Let's get this done with!" He went to the counter and picked up a tiny golden flask. "Here is the Elixir of Delight. I trust you have brought the antidote?"

Maximus Beedy smiled his thin, ugly smile. "Why, yes,"

he said, withdrawing a clear vial filled with a viscous black fluid from his trench coat.

The two men switched bottles. Maximus smiled unpleasantly. "Now drink up, Mr. Crackle, before you lose your eyes," he said.

Mr. Crackle held the bottle to the light and studied it. He gave it a swirl. His eyes darkened.

"Maximus Beedy, you may have fooled some fellows in your life, but never presume that you can fool an expert baker. I know exactly what is in this bottle, and it is not the antidote. You have given me liquefied poison-dart-frog toes. If I took it, I'd be a goner in three seconds."

"It doesn't matter now, does it?!" crowed Uncle Simon. "We've got the Elixir of Delight! Let's leave these miserable saps, Maximus, and make our fortune!"

Uncle Simon took a step toward the door. A cane whipped up and tapped him sharply on the belly.

Tap tap. Tap tap.

The cane swished down. It hit the tip of Uncle Simon's right shoe, then clicked onto the floor.

Uncle Simon yelped and jumped back. "Maximus! What the puffles are you doing?" he yelled.

Maximus Beedy moved in front of Simon, blocking his way to the door. He did not speak. He fixed an icy glare straight into Uncle Simon's eyes. His eyes did not blink.

Emma shuddered. There was something inhuman about his stillness.

Uncle Simon fell silent.

Maximus's thin voice floated through the air. "Simon Burblee, you are a complete and utter idiot. No criminal would trust this baker's word about the elixir. He gave it to us too easily. He did not fight. He did not demand the cure for the poison first. If he is clever enough to make the Elixir of Delight, then he is clever enough to trick us." He turned to Mr. Crackle. "What kind of game are you playing, Crackle?"

Mr. Crackle lifted one eyebrow. "Game?"

"Aha!" shouted Maximus. "You heard me, which means you've found a cure for my poison." He held up the elixir. "You're up to something with whatever's in this little flask, and I intend to find out what that something is." He turned to Uncle Simon. "You, Simon, must test the elixir."

"Me?!" squealed Emma's uncle. "Pig snouts and possum farts. Absolutely not. I'm not going to risk my neck so that you can get filthy rich."

Maximus's eyes glittered. "Oh, yes, you are, Simon. Do you remember that box of chocolates I offered you yesterday?"

"The ones I ate with the mashed liver?"

"Yes, the very ones. They were poisoned with a rather nasty concoction that will turn your insides to mud in"— Maximus casually glanced at the clock—"four hours and twelve minutes."

Uncle Simon went white. He gurgled. He tottered. His hand wobbled out to steady him and landed with a thump on the kitchen counter.

Maximus smiled contemptuously. "I will give you the antidote only after you try the elixir." He reached into his trench coat and pulled out a gleaming silver box. He opened it. Inside lay a sandwich.

Maximus said silkily, "Simon, I seem to recall you expressing a deep hatred of Brussels sprouts. As for me, I abhor anchovies. I've combined both ingredients into this disgusting morsel of food." He delicately removed the sandwich from the box.

Emma winced as she saw the sandwich stuffing—a purply green mash that was flecked with black and smelled faintly of the sewer.

Maximus plucked the tiny stopper off the elixir bottle. Holding the bottle above the sandwich, he tipped a drop of liquid onto the slimy mess and offered it to his partner. "Eat up! If the elixir works, it will be the most delicious thing you've ever tasted. If it doesn't, either our little baker has failed or else he has tricked us."

Uncle Simon slumped further and looked at Maximus with a horrified gaze.

"Personally," continued Maximus, "if I were him, I'd love to see you twisted up like a licorice stick, but who knows? Maybe our Mr. Crackle has succeeded. Anyhow, whether or not it works, I'll cure you of the chocolate poison afterward."

A horrible stillness filled the room. No one moved.

The only sound was the kitchen clock *tick-tick*ing, *tick-tick*ing.

There was one minute left before noon.

Suddenly Uncle Simon leaped up. He snatched the sandwich from Maximus and took one terrible, desperate bite. His bulging jaw worked up and down.

He swallowed.

And grinned.

His grin stretched wider and wider, until all his teeth showed. Bits of anchovy and Brussels sprouts stuck out from the gaps. "It worked!" he shouted. "Maximus, this is better than roasted pigs' feet! You have got to try it!" He took another enormous bite, then handed the rest to Maximus, who took a tiny nibble from the uneaten end.

The clock chimed noon.

32

The Anchovy and the Brussels Sprout

Uncle Simon gulped. Maximus Beedy swallowed.

They looked perfectly fine.

"Well, Mr. Crackle, it seems you have succeeded." Maximus took a silk handkerchief from his pocket and dabbed his mouth. "I detest anchovies, and yet this is the most exquisite sandwich I've ever tasted." He tucked the handkerchief back into his pocket. "Now, Simon, as for the antidote to the chocolates . . . Hold on, what the . . . ?"

Uncle Simon's head was changing. His skin had gone from pasty white to pale green. Veiny ridges crept up his bloated cheeks and curled around his head. His ears crinkled into round folds in his neck. His eyebrows disappeared into two leafy mounds.

Uncle Simon howled. His green eyes glazed with fury,

and he turned toward Maximus. His howl died with a choke.

Maximus Beedy's face had turned a scaly silver. His lips twisted into the shape of a beak, and his eyes grew three times their size. His entire head narrowed and sharpened.

In thirty seconds flat, Uncle Simon had turned into a Brussels sprout and Maximus Beedy had become a walking anchovy.

Mr. Crackle coughed. "So that's what happens when you drink the Elixir of Delight at noon. How interesting!"

"Crackle! You knew about this?!" roared the Brussels sprout.

It lurched toward Mr. Crackle, but before its leafy head could reach him, the anchovy darted forward and grabbed Emma with its fins.

Emma was buried in a mass of smelly fish scales. The fins were horribly sharp. One of them drew up an inch from her throat. She froze.

Maximus's voice came through the anchovy's gaping mouth. "Mr. Crackle, I think you should change us back at once. Otherwise, something unpleasant might happen."

Albie ran toward Emma but stopped short when the fish tightened its fin against her. "Leave Emma alone!" Albie yelled.

Mr. Crackle paled. For the first time since they had started this strange elixir-making, Emma could see he hadn't the foggiest idea what to do next.

The fin against her throat drew closer. Then Emma felt the razor edge of the fin brush against the hairs on her neck.

Suddenly she had a tiny spark of an idea.

"Mr. Crackle!" she gasped. "Just tell them where to get the cure! Tell them about the flour barrel!"

"What rubbish are you talking about?" hissed the fish.

"Get your fin away from me and I'll tell you!" Emma waited until the fin drew a fraction farther from her throat before she continued. "Mr. Crackle has a secret place where he stores all of his cures! Why do you think he hasn't died from that horrible poison yet? He showed me this place. You go down the flour barrel, then"—Emma made her voice a bit louder—"open a secret *door,* and inside are the cures to any problem you could think of!"

Mr. Crackle looked confused. For one awful moment, Emma was afraid he wouldn't understand.

Then an uncertain smile broke over his face.

"Yes, of course!" Mr. Crackle said. "Come with me, gentlemen, and I'll get you fixed right up."

He led everyone to the flour barrel, removed the cover, and flicked the wall switch. A whoosh of air flowed up and over the barrel. The soft glow of the tunnel lamps beckoned.

Mr. Crackle turned to Uncle Simon and Maximus and gestured toward the ladder. "Your antidote awaits below."

The anchovy snarled, "Crackle, you go down first. Simon goes next, then the boy, then Emma. I'll go last. Don't try anything funny."

Mr. Crackle got into the barrel and started to climb down. Emma watched her uncle flop his leafy arms onto the rungs of the ladder and follow. Albie gave her a quick hug, then dropped down.

The anchovy unwrapped its fins from around her. "Go," it said.

Emma swung her foot over the edge of the barrel.

Down, down, down.

Emma could hear Uncle Simon swearing as he struggled to descend in the body of a Brussels sprout. The rungs smelled faintly of rotten vegetables.

Deeper, deeper, deeper.

Then they were there.

✴33✴

Puffs of Green

The air was just as cool and the lamps just as friendly as Emma remembered. She clutched Mr. Crackle's and Albie's hands. Uncle Simon and Maximus scowled at the enormous door in front of them.

Emma stared at the door's wrought-iron handle and the breath box. She crossed her fingers.

"Crackle! Open this door at once!" barked Uncle Simon.

Mr. Crackle glanced at Emma, gave her hand a good squeeze, and took a deep breath. "Gentlemen, behind this door are my most precious ingredients and priceless recipes. I've protected it with a very special system. In order to go through, you must follow my directions exactly."

He approached the door and pointed to the glass pipe that led into the box full of metal loops. "I will blow through this tube, and on the count of three, all of us must push on the door together."

The Brussels sprout blundered to the door and gave it a suspicious look. "Why together?"

"If you touch it even a fraction of a second before I do, then the door will bounce you back like a sack of Jell-O." Mr. Crackle blew into the tube. "Ready? One, two . . . three!"

Maximus and Uncle Simon eagerly threw themselves against the door . . . just as Mr. Crackle, Emma, and Albie took a teeny step back.

CRACK! BANG!

Oily green smoke exploded into the tunnel. It smelled horribly of burned fish and vegetables. Emma began to sneeze and hack as her throat clogged. The tunnel swam before her eyes.

Behind her, Albie began to gurgle.

"Quickly!" cried Mr. Crackle. "Up the ladder!"

Emma dashed to the ladder. The rungs were slick with anchovy slime and stank terribly, but she gripped them tightly and raced up. Albie and Mr. Crackle followed right behind.

The foul smoke chased them, curling around Mr. Crackle's shoes.

Then his legs.

Then his neck.

"Hurry!" he gasped. "Hurry!"

Emma's fingers flew from rung to rung until at last she reached the top. With a mighty push, she dove out of the flour barrel. Albie launched himself over, and Mr. Crackle tumbled out after.

The smoke erupted from the barrel and flooded into the kitchen.

With Emma and Albie at his heels, Mr. Crackle ran to the front of the shop, wrenched open the door, and stumbled out.

"Whew!" wheezed Mr. Crackle. "What a smell!"

"Even my grandfather's toots aren't this bad!" gasped Albie.

Emma coughed and coughed out puffs of dark green smoke. With every cough, the puffs grew less green, until she was breathing only sweet, fresh outside air.

They waited until the smoke had cleared from the shop. Then they went back in.

Emma went to the flour barrel and peered down. She could still smell charred anchovy and Brussels sprout, and the lamps threw out a blurry greenish light, but not a trace of Maximus Beedy or Uncle Simon remained.

Mr. Crackle joined Emma at the barrel. "Goodness, that was exciting!"

Emma turned to Mr. Crackle. "Where do you think Mr. Beedy and Uncle Simon went?" she asked.

Mr. Crackle thought for a moment. "If I remember correctly, the king who turned into a lamb chop when he drank the Elixir of Delight at noon never turned back into his human form. I suppose your uncle and Maximus will forever be bits of smelly green smoke." He fanned the air with his broad hand. "It may take a few days for the odor to disappear, but soon enough there won't be a bit of your uncle or Maximus left."

"Good riddance!" cheered Albie. He kicked at a stray wisp of green smoke.

Emma smiled. For the first time that summer, she felt free.

Mr. Crackle reached for the wall switch. "Might as well air out the tunnel for a bit." But before his fingers closed on the switch, a gust of air swirled up through the tunnel.

"What the dickens? Someone must have turned the air current on from below!" Mr. Crackle cocked his head. "I wonder if it's Mabel. She might be wondering if everything turned out all right."

Sure enough, a few minutes later, Mabel's head poked out from the flour barrel. "Hello, Gregor," she said as she hoisted herself over the top. "I brought you some wicklewipes for the ghastly condition your ladder rungs are in."

"Mabel! How did you know I would need them?" Mr. Crackle yelped.

"When I left the spice shop this morning to go grocery shopping, I noticed a rather pungent odor in the air. On closer inspection, I discovered that it was coming from your tunnel. Really, Gregor," Mabel admonished, "you need to clean up after yourself. Other bakers need to use the main tunnel too!"

Mr. Crackle's shoulders slumped. "So you came up to

ask me to disinfect my ladder rungs, and not to see if I was all right?"

Mabel smiled very slightly. "Gregor Crackle, I had no doubt that you would get yourself out of your current pickle. But I do know that when something exciting happens, you tend to forget to pick up after yourself."

Emma started to giggle. Albie joined in, and although she did not laugh, Mabel looked at Mr. Crackle with a twinkle in her eye.

Mr. Crackle grinned ruefully. "Correct, as always, Mabel. I'll wicklewipe the ladder rungs clean today. If you're not too busy, could you lend a hand?"

"Gladly," Mabel said.

After the cleaning was done, Mr. Crackle baked a pizza for the four of them. As Mr. Crackle, Mabel, and Albie chatted and munched, Emma sat silent. During a pause in the conversation, Mabel gave Emma a concerned look. "Emma, what's wrong?"

"I guess now that Uncle Simon's gone, I'm going to have to call my parents and go back to the city." Emma stared mournfully at her green pepper and onion slice.

"Pish," said Mabel. "I've got a better idea. You've got a month left before school starts. Why don't you stay with me at the spice shop? I could use an assistant."

Emma stared at Mabel. A lovely tingle of happiness crept through her. "Really?"

"Of course," Mabel said warmly.

"Cross my buttons, that would be splendid!" Mr. Crackle crowed. "And you can help me in the kitchen whenever you want."

Emma gave a holler of joy.

"Well," said Mr. Crackle as the late-afternoon sun spilled into the kitchen, "I must ask you all for one more favor. My cake shop has been closed for two days, and I'm afraid my customers are going to be insatiable. Could you help me whip up some desserts for tomorrow?"

Albie jumped up. "Woo-hoo! Of course! What shall we make?"

Mr. Crackle grinned. "Have you ever tried babbleberry pie?"

"Didn't babbleberry juice turn all the Supreme-Extreme Masters into Popsicles?" asked Emma.

"Yes, but used properly, babbleberries make the best fruit desserts. Come, I'll show you."

And they began to hunt for mixing bowls and teaspoons.

✳ About the Author ✳

Meika Hashimoto attempted to make her first dessert, a basic chocolate cake, when she was eight. In her excitement, she forgot the sugar. And the baking powder. And she left the cake in the oven for far too long. Although it resembled a brick, her parents politely ate it. Meika's baking techniques have improved greatly since then. When she's not mixing batter or eating truffles, she can be found editing children's books.